ECHOES Of ENLIGHTENMENT

Discovering The Sacred World of Buddhist Art, Architecture and The Wisdom Within

DR. RAJKUMAR GADE

Clever Fox PUBLISHING
Chennai • Bangalore

CLEVER FOX PUBLISHING
Chennai, India

Published by CLEVER FOX PUBLISHING 2025

ISBN: 978-93-6707-715-3

CONTENTS

ABOUT THE AUTHOR

Rajkumar Gade is a distinguished author, humanitarian, engineer, artist, photographer, and sculptor whose profound passion for Buddhist heritage has shaped his work over the past two decades. He holds a doctorate in disaster management and is a civil engineer specializing in water resource management. In addition to his technical expertise, he is also a celebrated watercolor artist and sculptor, whose artistic lens brings a unique perspective to his explorations.

With an insatiable curiosity and a relentless pursuit of knowledge, he has travelled extensively across Afghanistan, China, Nepal, Bhutan, Vietnam, Cambodia, North Korea, Thailand, Indonesia, India, and Sri Lanka, immersing himself in the depths of Buddhist art, architecture, and philosophy. Through his journeys, he has engaged in discussions with thousands of people, gaining invaluable insights into their artistic traditions, engineering innovations, and cultural narratives.

Gade's work bridges multiple disciplines, combining engineering expertise with artistic expression and spiritual inquiry. His studies delve into the evolution of Buddhist architecture, construction techniques in monasteries and stupas, and the intricate symbolism of Buddhist iconography. His sculptural and photographic documentation captures the aesthetic and philosophical essence of Buddhist traditions, ensuring their preservation for future generations.

As an artist and sculptor, Gade has extensively explored Buddha's posture forms, Thangka paintings, Mandalas, and the impermanence of art, questioning how artistic expression conveys the deeper tenets of Buddhism. His critical analysis also examines the impact of political ideologies, and the decline of Buddhist art in India, shedding light on how Buddhist artistic traditions have been reshaped over time.

His research into Buddhist engineering Structures explores how ancient builders designed earthquake-resistant monasteries, sustainable water management systems, and grand temple complexes using sophisticated construction methods. His work on blueprints and design principles provides fresh insights into the architectural ingenuity of Buddhist structures in Southeast Asia.

Gade's rare ability to view Buddhist traditions through both artistic perspectives and engineering concepts sets his work apart. His keen observation skills, relentless questioning, and deep engagement with the communities he has encountered allow him to present a refreshing and multifaceted perspective on Buddhist heritage.

This book is a reflection of his twenty-year journey of exploration, documentation, and self-inquiry, a testament to his unwavering dedication to preserving and understanding the artistic and architectural wonders of Buddhism. His work is not just an academic endeavor but a deeply personal mission to bridge history, spirituality, and art into a unified narrative that transcends time.

Signature

SUMMARY

This book is a culmination of two decades of research, travel, and introspection by Rajkumar Gade, a distinguished author, humanitarian, engineer, artist, photographer, and sculptor. Through extensive journeys across Afghanistan, China, Nepal, Bhutan, Vietnam, Cambodia, North Korea, Thailand, Indonesia, India, and Sri Lanka, Gade has meticulously studied the rich heritage of Buddhist art, architecture, engineering, and philosophy.

The book explores the evolution of Buddhist artistic traditions, examining Buddha's postures, the significance of Mandalas and Thangka paintings, and their deeper philosophical meanings, particularly the concept of impermanence. It critically analyses the role of Buddhist engineering, detailing the construction techniques of monasteries, stupas, and massive temples across Southeast Asia, uncovering the secrets of their architectural resilience and spiritual symbolism.

Gade also investigates the decline of Buddhist artistic traditions in India, juxtaposing it with the continued vibrancy of Buddhist art in countries like Thailand, Cambodia, and China. The book delves into the Juche philosophy's impact on Buddhism in North Korea, highlighting how political ideologies have reshaped religious expression and artistic traditions.

With a keen eye for Buddha's head as a recurring artistic motif, the book discusses the ethical implications of disembodied sculptures and their commercialization in the modern world. It further examines Buddhist art's integration with local cultures in different countries, showcasing the cross-cultural adaptations that shaped iconography, architectural styles, and sculptural forms.

Gade's work is not just a study of Buddhist heritage but also an exploration of spirituality, artistic expression, and historical continuity. The book challenges conventional narratives, encouraging a deeper understanding of Buddhist aesthetics, the philosophy behind impermanence, and the transformative power of Buddhist art and architecture.

This is a monumental work that bridges history, art, engineering, and philosophy, offering fresh perspectives on Buddhist traditions while preserving their invaluable contributions to global heritage. Readers will find this book both enlightening and thought-provoking, as it sheds light on the enduring influence of Buddhist wisdom in shaping societies and artistic expressions across millennia.

PREFACE

Rajkumar Gade is an author, humanitarian, engineer, artist, photographer, and sculptor whose tireless pursuit of knowledge and understanding has shaped a monumental body of work over the past two decades. His extensive travels through Afghanistan, China, Nepal, Bhutan, Vietnam, Laos, Cambodia, North Korea, Thailand, Indonesia, India, and Sri Lanka have given him rare insights into Buddhist art, philosophy, engineering, and culture. With a deep sense of inquiry, he has dedicated himself to collecting and analysing information, constantly questioning the historical, artistic, and philosophical significance of Buddhist traditions across the world.

Gade's multidisciplinary expertise has allowed him to explore Buddhist heritage through engineering marvels, artistic expressions, and spiritual symbolism. His research delves into Buddhist architecture, engineering canons, sculpture, mandalas, thangka paintings, and the philosophical perspectives of Buddhism on art. He has meticulously documented the construction techniques of monasteries, stupas, and massive temples in Southeast Asia, tracing their influence through historical texts, oral traditions, and modern interpretations.

His work critically examines how Buddhism has shaped and been shaped by cultural, political, and ideological forces, including the impact of Juche philosophy in North Korea, the decline of Buddhist artistic traditions in India, and the evolution of Buddha's posture and iconography in different countries. Through his photography and sculpting, he has not only documented these elements but also created artistic expressions that bridge the past and present, offering a renewed appreciation of Buddhist aesthetics.

Rajkumar Gade's monumental journey is not merely an academic pursuit; it is a spiritual and artistic odyssey that seeks to uncover the essence of Buddhist wisdom through the tangible and intangible legacies left behind. His work challenges conventional narratives, shedding light on lost traditions, evolving artistic expressions, and the philosophical depths of Buddhist teachings. By bringing together art, architecture, engineering, and spirituality, his research stands as an invaluable contribution to the world of Buddhist studies.

This compilation of his work is a reflection of two decades of relentless exploration, meticulous documentation, and profound introspection. It invites readers to embark on a journey of discovery—one that traverses centuries of Buddhist heritage and questions the very nature of impermanence, devotion, and artistic ingenuity.

INTRODUCTION TO BUDDHIST ART AND PHILOSOPHY

Avalokiteshvara at Bouddha in Katmandu, Nepal

1

FROM SORROW TO SALVATION: HOW SUFFERING LED TO THE EVOLUTION AND SPREAD OF BUDDHISM IN DISASTER-PRONE REGIONS

The young prince gazed out from the gilded palace walls, his mind troubled by what lay beyond. Siddhartha Gautama had known only luxury, shielded from the realities of suffering by his father's insistence. But curiosity had led him beyond the gates, where he encountered the harsh truths of the world—an old man, a sick man, a corpse, and a wandering ascetic. In that moment, sorrow took root in his heart, a relentless question forming in his mind: Why do people suffer, and is there a way to end it?

This question led him on a journey that would change the world. Leaving behind his princely life, he wandered the forests, seeking wisdom from sages and ascetics. Yet, extreme austerities did not bring him peace. It was only under the Bodhi tree, after years of contemplation, that he discovered the Middle Path—the way to liberation from suffering. In that moment of enlightenment, the Four Noble Truths emerged like dawn breaking through the darkness:

1. Life is inherently filled with sorrow and dissatisfaction—**Dukkha**.
2. The cause of suffering is attachment and craving—**Samudaya**.
3. Liberation from suffering is possible—**Nirodha**.
4. The path to liberation lies in the Eightfold Path—**Magga**.

Siddhartha, now the Buddha, spent the rest of his life teaching this wisdom. And in the centuries that followed, his teachings spread—not just through peaceful lands, but through those battered by natural disasters, wars, and human suffering. In times of turmoil, people turned to Buddhism, drawn by its message of resilience, impermanence, and compassion.

Buddhism took root in India, Nepal, and Sri Lanka, where annual monsoons and droughts reminded people of life's fleeting nature. In China and Japan, where earthquakes and famine shaped history, Buddhist temples became shelters, offering solace to the suffering. In Myanmar and Thailand, where floods and cyclones swept through villages, Buddhist monks led relief efforts, reinforcing the importance of community and support. And in Tibet and the Himalayas, where life was a battle against the elements, Buddhist philosophy became intertwined with survival, guiding people to live in harmony with their harsh surroundings.

Everywhere Buddhism flourished, it adapted to the struggles of the people. In war-ravaged Cambodia and Vietnam, it became a force for healing and reconciliation. In the ancient monasteries of China, it preserved wisdom through centuries of upheaval. In the earthquake-prone lands of Japan, it taught acceptance of impermanence, reflected in the Zen gardens and the silent resilience of its people.

But Buddhism did not only comfort—it also rebuilt. Monasteries became hubs of humanitarian relief. The principles of **karuṇa** (compassion) and **Metta** (loving-kindness) fuelled efforts to help the wounded, the displaced, and the grieving. Meditation and mindfulness practices gave survivors tools to cope with trauma. The acceptance of impermanence allowed communities to move forward, not trapped by loss but inspired by renewal.

Even today, when earthquakes shake Nepal or tsunamis hit Sri Lanka, Buddhist monks are often among the first to respond. Their teachings, forged from the sorrow of a young prince thousands of years ago, remain as relevant as ever. The **Middle Path** was never just about enlightenment—it was about navigating suffering with wisdom, compassion, and resilience.

The journey from sorrow to salvation is not unique to Buddhism, but it is deeply embedded in its foundation. The Buddha himself was a seeker, a man who turned despair into a profound philosophy that still guides millions through disaster, loss, and change. His teachings do not promise to prevent suffering, but they illuminate a path through it—one of understanding, of peace, and of hope.

"The brush in a Buddhist artist's hand is not a mere tool, but an extension of their meditative mind, channelling mindfulness into every stroke."

2

BUDDHISM'S CONTRIBUTION TO WORLD PEACE: A STORY OF HARMONY AND RELEVANCE IN THE MODERN WORLD

The monk sat quietly under the Bodhi tree, his robes blending into the earth, his breath as steady as the river flowing nearby. He had walked through villages scarred by war, seen men and women cry over their losses, and yet, he carried no anger, no resentment—only peace. In his heart, he carried the words of the Buddha, passed down through generations, shaping the way humanity could heal itself from within.

Buddhism, from its very inception, was born not in the chaos of conquest but in the search for peace. When Siddhartha Gautama left his princely life behind, he did not seek dominion or power—he sought understanding. He saw suffering, felt its weight, and set out on a journey to unravel its cause and, most importantly, its resolution. What he discovered was a path not of aggression, but of balance—the **Middle Path**, a way of life that could transform societies, defuse tensions, and guide people away from the endless cycles of war and vengeance.

As Buddhism spread across Asia, it left behind not battlefields, but monasteries—centers of learning, sanctuaries of meditation, and strongholds of compassion. **Emperor Ashoka**, once a ruler of violence, was so profoundly transformed by the Buddha's teachings that he renounced war, choosing instead to carve pillars of peace throughout his empire. His message was simple yet revolutionary: true strength lies not in the sword, but in the ability to end suffering through wisdom and understanding.

Unlike many religions that became entangled with conquests, Buddhism did not march with armies. It traveled with pilgrims, merchants, and monks, reaching China, Japan, Sri Lanka, Tibet, and beyond. Along the Silk Road, in the mountains of the Himalayas, across the islands of Indonesia, Buddhism wove itself into diverse cultures, adapting but never losing its essence—peace, non-violence, and the boundless love of **Metta (Loving-Kindness)** and **Karuna (Compassion).**

In modern times, the echoes of Buddhist wisdom continue to shape movements for peace. **Thích Nhất Hạnh**, the Vietnamese monk who walked barefoot through war-torn villages, believed that peace was not just the absence of war but the presence of understanding. **The Dalai Lama**, despite the loss of his homeland, teaches compassion over retaliation. Even in societies far removed from traditional Buddhist lands, **mindfulness meditation**, rooted in ancient Buddhist thought, is used to reduce stress, heal trauma, and bring inner peace.

But Buddhism is not alone in seeking peace. **Christianity** speaks of love and forgiveness, yet history has seen wars waged in its name. **Islam**, in its essence, means peace, but political turmoil has sometimes overshadowed this truth. **Hinduism** embraces non-violence, inspiring figures like **Mahatma Gandhi**, while **Judaism** holds justice and peace as sacred. Yet, where other religions have been drawn into conflicts, Buddhism has largely remained untouched by religious warfare, offering a model of peace that the world continues to admire.

Today, in a world riddled with ideological divides, environmental crises, and rising tensions, Buddhist principles are more relevant than ever. Governments and peace negotiators use **Buddhist conflict resolution methods** to mediate tensions in Southeast Asia. **Mindfulness-based therapy** is now a cornerstone of mental health care, bringing healing to those affected by modern anxieties. Buddhist ethics remind us of our **interdependence with nature**, strengthening global movements for sustainability.

The old monk under the Bodhi tree slowly opened his eyes. Around him, the world was still restless, still filled with suffering. But he did not despair. For in the stillness of his breath, in the wisdom of the Buddha's words, he knew that the path to peace was always within reach. The challenge was not whether the world could find peace—but whether it was willing to walk the path toward it.

Buddhism does not promise an easy solution. It does not claim to erase suffering with mere belief. Instead, it offers something far more profound—a practice, a discipline, a way of being that, if followed with sincerity, can change not only individuals but entire civilizations. In the end, the greatest contribution of Buddhism to world peace is not its philosophy alone, but its unwavering belief in the potential of every person to choose compassion over conflict, understanding over division, and peace over war.

> "Buddhist art is not about preserving permanence, but about embodying the transient nature of existence, leaving an imprint on the soul rather than on time."

A women on Himalayas praying for world peace seen in the eye of an eagle

3

BUDDHA'S PERSPECTIVE ON ART: A JOURNEY THROUGH TIME

The monk sat in the shade of the Bodhi tree, his robe folded neatly over his legs, eyes closed in deep meditation. Around him, his disciples listened to the wind rustling through the leaves, the soft whisper of the universe in motion. For years, the Buddha had walked from village to village, speaking not of form and beauty, but of suffering and the impermanence of all things. To him, the pursuit of art, like the pursuit of wealth or pleasure, was another attachment—one more tether binding souls to the cycle of birth and rebirth.

Yet, as centuries passed, his words transformed not only hearts but hands. The great kings and followers who carried his teachings across vast lands did not speak only with words, but with chisels on stone, colors on walls, and gold on statues. In the beginning, they dared not depict him in human form. Instead, they carved the Dharma Wheel, the sacred Bodhi tree, or the footprints he left behind, symbols that spoke of his presence without confining him to an earthly figure.

Then came the era of change. In the distant lands of Gandhara, where Greek sculptors met Buddhist monks, a new image was born. The Buddha, once formless, now stood with serene grace, draped in flowing robes, his face sculpted with divine stillness. His eyes, half-closed in eternal wisdom, gazed upon the world—not as a man of flesh and blood, but as an idea, a guide, a reminder of the path to liberation.

In India, the murals of Ajanta sprang to life with the stories of his past lives, the Jataka tales, painted on stone walls with delicate hands. In Tibet, thangka paintings wove intricate cosmic visions, meditative tools leading the faithful deeper into the nature of existence. In each stroke of color and curve of sculpture, a truth was whispered: nothing is permanent, not even the art that sought to immortalize him.

In faraway temples, artisans devoted lifetimes to carving his image into mountain rock faces and towering stupas. In Burma, in Cambodia, in Japan—each culture painted him in their own vision, not changing his essence, but reflecting their own. In the snowy monasteries of the Himalayas, monks meticulously crafted sand mandalas, only to brush them away once completed, an act that embodied the very heart of his teachings: beauty, like life, must dissolve back into the universe.

Perhaps the Buddha never spoke of art because he knew its paradox—how could something so impermanent be used to represent the timeless truth of enlightenment? And yet, through these expressions, his message lived on. His image, once avoided, now became the universal face of compassion, teaching millions in silence, long after his voice had faded into history.

Even today, in museums, in sacred halls, and in bustling markets where statues of him are bought and sold, his gaze remains the same—unmoved, unwavering. Perhaps he understood, more than anyone, that art was never about permanence. It was always about the message it carried, and the hands that shaped it with reverence, before letting it go.

> "Every chisel mark on stone is a whisper of devotion, a dialogue between the artist and eternity, capturing impermanence within permanence."

A Thangka Painting carrying legacy of centuries of artform

4

BUDDHA'S HEAD AS AN ARTISTIC SYMBOL: A STORY OF REVERENCE AND CONTROVERSY

The artisan's chisel moved with slow, deliberate strokes, revealing the serene face of the Buddha from a block of stone. His fingers traced the outline of the ushnisha, the cranial protuberance that symbolized boundless wisdom. For him, this was not merely an artistic endeavour—it was an act of devotion. Yet, beyond the quiet sanctuary of his workshop, the world had transformed Buddha's head into something else entirely. Displayed in modern homes, luxury hotels, and fashion boutiques, the disembodied Buddha had become an aesthetic commodity, its spiritual essence often overshadowed by commercial appeal.

A Sacred Symbol Turned Icon of Modernity

Once, Buddhist artisans crafted statues as complete entities—the whole form of the Buddha seated in meditation, walking in grace, or reclining in serene departure. The head was never meant to be isolated, for the Buddha's teachings encompassed the entirety of existence, not fragmented pieces of it. Yet today, the head alone is showcased, removed from its spiritual context, admired for its tranquil expression but often devoid of meaning.

How did it come to this?

The earliest depictions of the Buddha in Gandhara, Mathura, and Southeast Asia presented him in full-bodied glory—a teacher, a guide, an enlightened being in physical and spiritual form. The idea of portraying only his head did not exist in classical Buddhist traditions. This fragmentation began when colonial expeditions and art collectors sought portable relics, removing heads from full statues to display them in Western museums and galleries. What was once an object of veneration became a prized collectible, severed from its roots.

The Ethical Quandary: Art or Appropriation?

As centuries passed, Buddha's head became an increasingly familiar sight outside temples and shrines. Carved into fountains, embedded in gardens, printed onto t-shirts, even transformed into candle holders—its sacred essence diluted by mass production.

In many Buddhist cultures, the head is the most revered part of the body, to be touched only in reverence, not removed from its whole. Yet, in modern consumerism, it has been detached, displayed, and sold, often by those with no understanding of its spiritual significance.

Governments in Thailand, Sri Lanka, and Myanmar have spoken against this practice. Campaigns have emerged, reminding people that placing a Buddha's head as a decorative piece in a bar or spa disrespects its sanctity. Temples have put up signs pleading with tourists not to take selfies with Buddha statues. For the faithful, such uses are not mere artistic liberties—they are acts of disregard.

An Artist's Dilemma: Where Does Respect End and Creativity Begin?

The debate rages on. Artists argue that depicting the Buddha's head is a form of homage, a way to bring his teachings into contemporary spaces. They believe that in carving his likeness, they extend his presence into new realms of understanding. Yet, context matters. A sculpture placed in a temple or a museum, with proper reverence and explanation, is different from a mass-produced golden head displayed next to a neon-lit bar counter.

One sculptor, struggling with this dilemma, spoke of the weight he felt when creating Buddha's image. "If I carve only his head, am I honoring him, or am I reducing him?" The question lingered in his heart. Perhaps the true answer lay not in the act itself, but in the intention behind it.

Finding Balance: A Call for Mindfulness

As the world grows more interconnected, cultural appreciation must tread carefully between reverence and appropriation. The Buddha's image is not just an artistic motif—it is a living symbol of peace, wisdom, and enlightenment for millions.

What, then, is the way forward?

- Full-body depictions remain the most respectful in Buddhist traditions.
- Museums and collectors must ensure that artifacts, especially Buddha heads, are sourced ethically and displayed with proper historical context.
- Those who use Buddha's image in décor and art should understand its significance and avoid trivializing it.

A Legacy Beyond Stone

As the sculptor set down his chisel, he took a step back and looked at the face he had brought to life. Would his creation be honored, or would it become just another decoration, stripped of its depth?

The fate of Buddhist art, like the Buddha's teachings themselves, depended on those who encountered it. Would they see only a face, or would they recognize the wisdom behind the eyes?

> "The posture of the Buddha in sculpture is not just a pose; it is a manifestation of inner balance, wisdom, and the journey toward enlightenment."

Boddhisatva Padmapani- The lotus bearer

5

HOW INDIA LOST ITS PROMINENCE IN BUDDHIST ART: A STORY OF FORGOTTEN GLORY

The sun hung low over the ruins of Nalanda, casting elongated shadows over the ancient bricks that once housed the greatest Buddhist scholars of their time. The wind carried whispers of forgotten chants, prayers that had once echoed within these sacred halls. India—the very land where the Buddha had walked, where the Dharma had flourished, where artists had sculpted enlightenment into stone—had lost its claim to Buddhist art.

The Rise and Fall of Buddhist Art in India

For centuries, Buddhist monks and artisans worked side by side, chiseling divine figures into caves, painting celestial scenes onto monastery walls, and erecting stupas that reached toward the sky. From Sanchi to Ajanta, from Amaravati to Bodh Gaya, India's artistic brilliance was unparalleled. The world looked to India for inspiration, and the Silk Road carried its influence far and wide. But as time unfolded, the golden age of Buddhist art began to fade.

The shift was gradual at first. During the Maurya and Gupta dynasties, Buddhism thrived, supported by emperors who saw wisdom in its teachings. The Gupta Empire (4th-6th century CE), in particular, became a beacon of Buddhist artistic expression, refining sculpture, architecture, and painting to new levels of sophistication. Ajanta's murals glowed with spiritual devotion, and Nalanda became a hub of Buddhist thought and artistic innovation.

Then, change came—not in the form of war or sudden destruction, but as a quiet shift in devotion. Hinduism began to reclaim its dominance, and the kings who once adorned Buddhist monasteries with wealth and artistic patronage turned their focus to Hindu temple-building traditions. The magnificent temples of Ellora and Khajuraho emerged, their towering spires dedicated to Shiva and Vishnu. The Bhakti movement swept across India, drawing people back to the deities of old, and in its wake, Buddhist monasteries fell into neglect. The hands that once carved the compassionate Buddha now shaped gods of war and love.

Invasions and the Fall of Buddhist Institutions

Yet, Buddhism might have survived, clinging to its dwindling corners in India—if not for the violent upheavals that followed. In the 12th century, Islamic invasions brought destruction to some of the most revered Buddhist centers. The universities of

Nalanda and Vikramashila, where artists and monks had trained for generations, were burned to the ground. The invaders saw the grand stupas and monasteries as symbols of a past they wished to erase. Libraries filled with Buddhist manuscripts became ash, and sculptures that once exuded serenity were shattered beneath the force of conquest.

While Hinduism adapted to new rulers and blended with Islamic art forms, Buddhism in India had no political defenders left. It retreated into the shadows, while in the east, its legacy found a new home.

Buddhism's Journey Beyond India

Even as Buddhism withered in its birthplace, its artistic legacy flourished elsewhere. The monks who once studied in India traveled to China, Japan, and Southeast Asia, carrying with them artistic techniques, scriptures, and relics. In Dunhuang, Chinese artists expanded upon the techniques of Ajanta, crafting murals that would dazzle the world. In Japan, Buddhist iconography merged with Zen simplicity, birthing masterpieces of meditation and minimalism. In Thailand and Myanmar, gilded Buddha statues and golden temples replaced the sandstone stupas of India.

The teachings of the Buddha endured, but in foreign hands, they evolved into new artistic traditions. Gandhara's Greco-Buddhist sculptures became the foundation of Buddhist art in Afghanistan and Central Asia. The intricate mandalas and thangka paintings of Tibet took on new spiritual significance. What India had lost, the world had embraced.

A Revival, but a Silent One

Centuries later, in the 19th and 20th centuries, India rediscovered its Buddhist past. The ruins of Sanchi and Ajanta were unearthed, scholars and historians marveled at the forgotten grandeur, and leaders like Dr. B.R. Ambedkar championed a revival of Buddhism among India's Dalit communities. Yet, the artistic traditions that once defined Buddhist India never fully returned.

The stupas still stand, the cave paintings still whisper their ancient tales, but they are monuments of history rather than living centers of artistic innovation. Meanwhile, in China, Japan, Thailand, and Myanmar, Buddhist art continued to evolve, to flourish, to redefine itself for new generations.

A Legacy in Stone and Silence

As the monk walked through the deserted ruins of Nalanda, he paused before a fallen statue of the Buddha, its features worn by time, its hands still raised in a gesture of peace. India had given Buddhism to the world—but had let its artistic soul slip away.

And yet, the story was not over. The murals of Ajanta still drew scholars from around the globe, the great stupas still stood tall against the sky, and in quiet corners, artists still painted the Buddha's serene face, as they had done for centuries. India may no longer be the heart of Buddhist art, but its pulse still beats in the echoes of stone and the whispers of ancient brushstrokes.

> "For the past is never truly lost. It waits, in silence, to be remembered"

A lady in a deep meditation while spinning the Buddhist Mantra wheel

EVOLUTION OF BUDDHIST ARTISTIC EXPRESSIONS

6

BUDDHA'S POSTURE FORMS: A SCULPTOR'S JOURNEY THROUGH THEIR VARIED INTERPRETATIONS ACROSS CULTURES

The chisel struck the stone with rhythmic precision, each stroke guided by centuries of tradition. As the sculptor stepped back, a serene face emerged, its features imbued with a sense of deep contemplation. This was not just a statue—it was a manifestation of enlightenment, shaped by hands that had inherited the legacy of countless artisans before them. Across the world, from India to Japan, from Cambodia to China, the depiction of the Buddha had evolved, taking on different postures, expressions, and styles. Each carving told a story—not just of faith, but of history, culture, and artistic interpretation.

The Classical Origins: India's Sculptural Foundations

In the ancient caves of Ajanta and Ellora, the earliest depictions of the Buddha took form. India, the birthplace of Buddhism, established the foundational artistic vocabulary—standing figures in Abhaya Mudra, their raised hands symbolizing reassurance and fearlessness; seated figures in Dhyana Mudra, lost in meditation; and the serene yet sorrowful Reclining Buddha, depicting his final moments before entering Nirvana. These forms, etched into stone, became the prototypes for Buddhist art across Asia. Every posture held meaning, every gesture a lesson in spiritual wisdom.

Gandhara's Greco-Buddhist Fusion: When East Met West

As Buddhism traveled north into Gandhara (modern-day Pakistan and Afghanistan), it met the influence of Greek sculptural traditions. The result? A breathtaking fusion of Hellenistic realism and Indian spirituality. The Buddha of Gandhara bore wavy hair, deep-set eyes, and togas reminiscent of Roman emperors. For the first time, Buddhist figures adopted the contrapposto stance, a dynamic posture that imbued statues with a sense of movement and life. Here, the Buddha was not just an idea but a living presence, carved with the precision of Western realism yet filled with Eastern mysticism.

China's Elegant and Symbolic Approach

Further east, in the vast landscapes of China, Buddhism intertwined with Confucian ideals of harmony and grace.

Sculptors in Longmen and Dunhuang adorned temple walls with Buddhas seated in the Earth-Touching Posture (Bhumisparsha Mudra), signifying the moment of enlightenment. Avalokiteshvara Bodhisattva (Guanyin), depicted with delicate features and flowing robes, became a symbol of boundless compassion. The Chinese Buddhas often had elongated, ethereal proportions, reinforcing their divine and otherworldly presence, in contrast to the more human-like depictions of India and Gandhara.

Japan's Zen Minimalism and Dynamic Forms

In Japan, Buddhist sculpture evolved with a distinct sense of minimalism and tranquility. The Amida Buddha, seated in Dhyana Mudra, was crafted with exquisite simplicity, found in temples such as Byodoin's Phoenix Hall. Unlike the stillness of seated Buddhas elsewhere, Japan also introduced the Walking Buddha, a rare form seen in the Heian and Kamakura periods, capturing fluidity and motion. Jizo Bodhisattva, standing guard along roadsides, embodied protection and kindness, particularly for children and travelers. Here, Buddhist sculpture was not just an artistic endeavor—it was an emotional connection between the divine and the earthly.

Thailand and Southeast Asia: Grace in Motion

In Thailand, Myanmar, and Cambodia, the Buddha was depicted with an unparalleled sense of grace and dynamism. The Walking Buddha (Tribhanga Pose), unique to Thailand, symbolized the Buddha in mid-stride, as if guiding devotees forward. The Maravijaya Buddha (Subduing Mara Pose), one hand touching the earth in defiance of temptation, became a dominant image across Thai temples. Meanwhile, the colossal Reclining Buddhas of Wat Pho (Bangkok) and Bagan (Myanmar) presented the moment of enlightenment on an almost celestial scale. Buddhist sculpture here was not just an artistic expression—it was an immersive experience, grand in scale and divine in presence.

Tibetan Vajrayana and Esoteric Interpretations

High in the Himalayas, Buddhist sculpture took on an esoteric dimension. Tibetan art, infused with Tantric symbolism, portrayed the Buddha in powerful and intricate forms. Yab-Yum depictions symbolized the cosmic union of wisdom and compassion. Dharmapalas, fierce guardian deities, stood with fire in their eyes, protecting the Dharma from corruption. Mandala-based sculptures, meticulously crafted, represented the universe itself, a visual meditation on the nature of existence. Here, the Buddha was more than a teacher—he was a force, an energy, a cosmic truth embodied in form.

Cambodia's Unique Blend of Hindu-Buddhist Art

In the sprawling temples of Angkor Wat and Bayon, Buddhist and Hindu influences merged in mesmerizing harmony. The Bayon Buddha faces, their tranquil smiles gazing in all directions, represented the omnipresent Avalokiteshvara, embodying universal compassion. The Mucalinda Buddha, seated beneath the sheltering hood of a seven-headed serpent, symbolized the protective embrace of nature itself. Cambodian sculptors wove spirituality into their art, transforming temple walls into cosmic canvases of divine storytelling.

Myanmar's Monumental Buddhas: Devotion in Scale

Few places celebrate Buddha's presence on a grander scale than Myanmar. Here, entire landscapes are dominated by colossal statues—the Shwethalyaung Reclining Buddha in Bago, stretching 55 meters in length, and the golden Mahamuni Buddha in Mandalay, whose form is continuously coated in layers of gold leaf by devoted pilgrims. The sheer size of these sculptures is not just an artistic choice—it is a declaration of faith, a tangible embodiment of Buddhist devotion.

Vietnam's Harmonization of Traditions

In Vietnam, Buddhist sculpture absorbed elements from China, India, and indigenous traditions, creating a unique visual language. The Quan Am Bodhisattva (Vietnamese Avalokiteshvara) took on a graceful, feminine form, emphasizing boundless mercy. The Seated Lotus Buddha, found in temples like the One Pillar Pagoda in Hanoi, symbolized stability and peace. Meanwhile, the laughing Maitreya Buddha, depicted with a wide smile and a round belly, reflected a vision of happiness and abundance. Vietnamese Buddhist art was about balance—between past and present, between wisdom and joy.

The Ever-Evolving Legacy of Buddhist Sculpture

As the sculptor stepped back from his work, he marveled at the figure before him—a seated Buddha, hands folded in meditation, his face exuding infinite calm. Though shaped by his hands, this form was not his alone—it was the inheritance of thousands before him, the echoes of India, Gandhara, China, Japan, Thailand, Cambodia, and beyond.

Buddha's postures, though varied across cultures, all spoke the same silent truth—a testament to peace, wisdom, and the eternal journey toward enlightenment. As long as sculptors continued to carve, paint, and mold, the Buddha would remain, not just in temples and shrines, but in the very soul of humanity itself.

A painting of Buddha idol worshipping

7

GANDHARA SCHOOL OF BUDDHISM: A TALE OF CULTURAL CONFLUENCE IN STONE AND SPIRIT

The sculptor wiped the sweat from his brow, his chisel poised against the cool grey schist. Before him, a block of stone waited to become something greater—a form that would merge the wisdom of the East with the refinement of the West. As he carved, the features of a serene Buddha emerged, his robes cascading in deep folds, his hair curled in Greco-Roman fashion, his expression imbued with the infinite calm of enlightenment. In that moment, history itself was being written in stone.

The Gandhara School of Buddhist art, which flourished between the 1st century BCE and the 5th century CE in what is now Afghanistan and Pakistan, was a marvel of artistic fusion. This was not just a local tradition—it was the outcome of an extraordinary cultural crossroads. Here, Greek sculptural realism, Roman architectural grandeur, Persian motifs, and Indian spiritual symbolism blended seamlessly, shaping an artistic revolution that would resonate across Asia for centuries to come.

The Birth of an Artistic Renaissance

It began with the echoes of Alexander the Great's conquests in the 4th century BCE, as Greek artistic traditions made their way deep into Central and South Asia. The Bactrian kings, inheritors of this Greco-Macedonian influence, fostered an environment where classical aesthetics flourished alongside the growing spread of Buddhism. The gods of Olympus faded, replaced by the meditative stillness of the Buddha—but his form, for the first time, bore the hallmarks of Hellenistic grace.

In Gandhara, sculptors abandoned the early Indian tradition of depicting the Buddha symbolically—as a tree, a footprint, or an empty throne. Instead, inspired by Greek statues of Apollo and Zeus, they humanized the Buddha, sculpting him with high cheekbones, expressive eyes, and a commanding yet compassionate presence. His flowing robes, reminiscent of Roman togas, were carved with meticulous detail, creating an illusion of weight and movement never before seen in Buddhist art.

The sculptors of Gandhara did not merely copy Greek aesthetics; they transformed them. They infused Buddhist ideals into classical forms, crafting an entirely new artistic language. The realistic musculature of a Greek athlete became the poised, meditative stillness of a Buddha in deep contemplation. The Corinthian columns of Western temples found new purpose in Buddhist stupas and monastic gateways. The result was an art form that retained its European refinement while expressing the profound spirituality of the East.

Sculpting the Future: The Spread of Gandhara's Influence

As trade flourished along the Silk Road, Gandhara's artistic innovations journeyed far beyond their homeland. Chinese pilgrims, traveling to learn the teachings of the Buddha, encountered the grandeur of Taxila, Bamiyan, and Peshawar, where colossal Buddhas stood as silent sentinels of faith. They carried home not only scriptures but artistic inspiration, introducing Gandhara's three-dimensional realism into the murals of Dunhuang in China and the temple carvings of Nara in Japan.

Even in Indonesia, the vast stone reliefs of Borobudur echo the visual storytelling of Gandhara, their figures rendered with the same depth and naturalism. The Bamiyan Buddhas, towering over 50 meters in the Afghan cliffs, stood as the ultimate embodiment of Gandhara's global legacy—an artistic testament to a civilization that connected Rome to India, Greece to China, Persia to Japan.

A Legacy in Stone, a Legacy at Risk

For centuries, Gandhara's masterpieces endured—silent but eternal. However, time was not always kind. The Bamiyan Buddhas, once the pride of Afghanistan, were destroyed in 2001, their grandeur reduced to dust. Yet, the spirit of Gandhara remains unbroken. Its legacy is preserved in the sculptures housed in museums, in the stylistic echoes found in Buddhist art across

Asia, and in the unwavering reverence for a school of art that bridged worlds and reshaped civilizations.

As the last chips of stone fell from his chisel, the sculptor stepped back, gazing at the form he had brought to life. The folds of the Buddha's robe danced with light and shadow, his face radiated serenity, his presence was timeless. It was a masterpiece born of two worlds—a testament to the enduring power of cultural synthesis, of art as a universal language. In Gandhara, East and West were no longer separate—they were one, carved into the very fabric of time.

> "Gandhara art was where Eastern spirituality met Western realism—not in opposition, but in a harmonious convergence of form and philosophy."

8

THE INFLUENCE OF BUDDHIST ART ON CAMBODIAN ARCHITECTURE: A STORY OF SACRED TRANSFORMATION

The dense jungle hummed with life as the first rays of dawn illuminated the towering spires of Angkor Wat. The temple's reflection shimmered in the still waters of the moat, as if the divine and earthly realms had momentarily fused. A lone monk, clad in saffron robes, walked barefoot along the ancient causeway, his presence a testament to the silent dialogue between past and present. The stones beneath his feet held stories of kings and gods, of wars and prayers, of an empire that once stood as the pinnacle of spiritual and artistic grandeur. And at the heart of it all was the fusion of Hindu and Buddhist art, woven into the very fabric of Cambodia's architectural legacy.

For centuries, the Khmer Empire had been devoted to the gods of Hinduism. Its rulers built magnificent temples in honor of

Vishnu and Shiva, carving epic tales of the Ramayana and Mahabharata into temple walls, immortalizing their devotion in stone. But then came a change—a shift in belief, a new spiritual path that would reshape the artistic soul of Cambodia.

A Kingdom in Transition: The Rise of Buddhist Influence

As the 12th century unfolded, a powerful ruler ascended the throne—King Jayavarman VII, a devout follower of Mahayana Buddhism. Under his reign, Buddhism became the state religion, altering not just the faith of the Khmer people but the very essence of their temples. The divine faces of Hindu gods gave way to the serene visage of the Buddha; temple halls once filled with depictions of celestial battles now portrayed the simple, compassionate teachings of enlightenment. The temples themselves did not fall, but they adapted, evolving into sacred spaces where both religions coexisted in stone.

Angkor Wat: A Hindu Monument Embracing Buddhist Influence

Built in the early 12th century by King Suryavarman II, Angkor Wat was originally conceived as a grand tribute to Vishnu, its soaring towers symbolizing Mount Meru, the center of the universe in Hindu cosmology. The temple's bas-reliefs teemed with Hindu mythology—churning oceans of milk, celestial nymphs dancing in divine ecstasy, warriors locked in eternal battle.

But as centuries passed, Buddhism took root in the Khmer heartland, and Angkor Wat gradually transformed. Buddhist monks adopted the temple as a place of meditation, adding statues of the Buddha within its sacred corridors. Hindu deities were not erased but reinterpreted, seamlessly blending two faiths into one architectural masterpiece. Today, as visitors walk through Angkor's galleries, they witness an artistic dialogue between the two traditions—a past that did not die, but evolved.

Bayon Temple: The Face of Buddhist Cambodia

In the heart of Angkor Thom, another marvel rose under Jayavarman VII's vision—Bayon Temple, a profound expression of Mahayana Buddhist influence. Unlike Angkor Wat, Bayon was built from its very inception as a Buddhist sanctuary. Its most striking feature? Over 200 colossal stone faces gazing in quiet contemplation over the kingdom.

Scholars debate whether these faces represent Avalokiteshvara, the Bodhisattva of Compassion, or Jayavarman VII himself, immortalized as a benevolent ruler overseeing his people. The temple's walls tell a different story than those of Hindu temples—here, instead of gods waging war, we see glimpses of everyday Khmer life—fishermen casting their nets, market vendors selling goods, warriors marching alongside elephants. The shift was profound—art no longer glorified only the divine but also honored the human experience.

Ta Prohm and the Living Temples of Buddhism

There is another place where the embrace of Buddhism remains undeniable—Ta Prohm, the temple reclaimed by nature. Built as a Buddhist monastery, its walls were once adorned with images of Prajnaparamita, the Goddess of Wisdom, reflecting the deep philosophical underpinnings of Buddhist teachings. Even as later rulers attempted to erase Buddhist symbols during Hindu revivals, many carvings survived, their softened forms whispering stories of a past where both traditions coexisted.

Here, nature and stone engage in an eternal dance—roots of ancient trees embrace the temple walls, as if the forest itself is safeguarding the last remnants of Cambodia's Buddhist heritage.

The Artistic Confluence of Hinduism and Buddhism

The beauty of Khmer architecture lies in its ability to blend faiths, rather than erase them. As Buddhism flourished, Hindu iconography was not eradicated but adapted. Hindu deities were carved with serene expressions, their poses resembling the meditative stillness of the Buddha. The rigid forms of Hindu art softened under Buddhist influence, giving birth to a style that celebrated both the cosmic and the earthly, the divine and the human.

Khmer sculptors, once trained in the dramatic energy of Hindu gods, turned their chisels towards crafting gentle Bodhisattvas, tranquil Buddhas, and celestial beings that radiated wisdom rather than power. Their hands, instead of holding weapons, now formed mudras, gestures of enlightenment and compassion.

A Legacy Carved in Stone

Today, Angkor Wat, Bayon, and Cambodia's many temples stand as echoes of this remarkable confluence, where art was not bound by singular belief but enriched by many. Their walls tell the tale of a civilization that embraced transformation, not as destruction, but as evolution.

As the monk walked through the temple grounds, his fingers lightly brushed against the ancient carvings. He knew that what lay beneath his touch was more than stone—it was history, faith, and an enduring testament to the power of artistic and spiritual unity. For in Cambodia's temples, one does not simply witness the past; one steps into a world where Hindu and Buddhist art breathe as one.

The grand Angkorwat Temple in Cambodia

9

AJANTA FRESCOS: A LEGACY CARVED IN STONE AND COLOR

The cool darkness of the cave provided refuge from the blazing Indian sun. A flickering oil lamp cast long, wavering shadows on the walls as a young apprentice watched his master at work. He held his breath, mesmerized, as the old painter moved his brush with effortless grace, bringing life to stone. The walls of Ajanta, once mere rock, were now portals to another world—a world where stories of gods, kings, and ordinary men unfolded in waves of color and form.

It was in the 2nd century BCE that Buddhist monks first sought sanctuary in these cliffs of Maharashtra, carving hidden temples into their embrace. But these were no mere shelters; they were places where devotion took shape, where enlightenment was pursued not just through meditation but through art. And so, artists, commissioned by patrons of faith and royalty, transformed these stone chambers into masterpieces of storytelling, emotion, and divine beauty.

With each brushstroke, an era was immortalized. The Jataka tales, the sacred stories of Buddha's past lives, were etched into the very soul of the caves. These were not simple illustrations but living expressions—scenes of love, sorrow, sacrifice, and triumph, painted with such delicacy that they spoke directly to the heart. Each face, every glance, every flowing garment carried meaning, capturing the essence of human experience in a way the world had never seen before.

The technique was revolutionary. The artists did not merely paint on stone—they made the stone itself part of the composition. Using natural pigments ground from minerals, plants, and shells, they mixed colors that sank deep into the damp plaster, fusing with the walls as if they had always belonged there. This technique, predating European frescoes by over a thousand years, ensured that the hues remained vibrant even after centuries of neglect.

But what truly set Ajanta apart was its profound understanding of depth and perspective. Long before the Renaissance, these artists manipulated light and shadow, creating illusions of movement, volume, and space. Figures leaned into conversations, their robes flowing as though stirred by an unseen breeze. Eyes gleamed with life, expressions shifting subtly with the play of torchlight.

The influence of Ajanta did not remain confined within these caves. As traders and pilgrims carried Buddhist teachings across the Silk Road, the style of these frescos found echoes in the murals of Dunhuang in China, the temples of Borobudur in Indonesia, and even in Persian and Byzantine miniature paintings. The whispers of Ajanta's artists found their way into the hands of unknown masters across Asia, shaping the very foundation of religious and narrative art in distant lands.

Centuries later, when European explorers and art historians stumbled upon these hidden wonders, they were astounded. Some saw echoes of Ajanta's fluid forms in Renaissance compositions, its shading and realism akin to the work of Leonardo da Vinci and Michelangelo. The caves, long abandoned and overgrown, reemerged into the world's consciousness, standing as testaments to India's artistic and spiritual grandeur.

Today, visitors step into these caves as if entering a sacred dream. The frescos whisper their ancient stories, their colors still radiant despite time's relentless march. Conservators work tirelessly to protect these fragile visions, aware that they hold something priceless—not just paint and plaster, but the very soul of a civilization, etched in time.

In the grand tapestry of world art, the Ajanta frescos remain unparalleled. They are more than paintings—they are a bridge across millennia, a conversation between past and present, an eternal flame illuminating the boundless reach of human creativity. As long as there are eyes to see and hearts to feel, Ajanta will live on, its beauty undimmed, its stories forever unfolding in the silent embrace of stone.

> *"The frescos of Ajanta are not just paintings; they are visual scriptures, whispering the dharma across centuries, keeping the Jataka tales alive."*

10

THE MYSTIC BRUSHSTROKES: THE RISE OF TANTRISM IN BUDDHIST ART ACROSS NEPAL, BHUTAN, TIBET, AND LADAKH

The monastery perched on the edge of a windswept cliff, its golden rooftop glinting under the first light of dawn. The scent of burning juniper filled the air, mingling with the faint echoes of distant chants that seemed to rise and fall with the mountains themselves. Inside the dimly lit temple, a young monk knelt before an unfinished thangka painting, his brush poised above the delicate silk. His hands trembled slightly as he traced the outline of a wrathful deity, the guardian of wisdom and protector of the Dharma.

His master, an aged lama whose eyes had seen many lifetimes pass in the flicker of butter lamps, watched him with quiet patience. Finally, he spoke. "Do you know what you are painting?"

The monk hesitated, his gaze lingering on the fierce figure taking form beneath his brush. "A protector of the Dharma," he whispered. "A being of great Tantric power."

The master nodded approvingly. "Yes, but it is also a gateway—a reflection of the hidden truths that lie beyond form, beyond color, beyond this world." He moved closer, the rich folds of his maroon robe rustling like old parchment. "Let me tell you how this art came to be."

The Birth of Tantrism in Buddhist Art

Long ago, Buddhism was a path of simplicity—a gentle river leading seekers toward enlightenment. But in the secret depths of India's forests, in the echoing chambers of hidden caves, a different current began to stir. Tantric Buddhism, or Vajrayana, was unlike anything before it.

Here, enlightenment was not something to be reached through lifetimes of slow practice. It was immediate, electric, like a bolt of lightning igniting the soul. Those who followed this path used visualization, mantras, and powerful rituals to channel divine energy, transforming themselves into living mandalas of enlightenment.

And art—art became the vessel through which these mysteries were revealed. No longer was the Buddha depicted solely in serene meditation. Now, he appeared adorned with jewels, encircled by cosmic flames, his body a fusion of wisdom and compassion. The gods and demons of the old world did not vanish; they too were transformed, reborn as protectors of the Dharma, forces of both destruction and creation.

The young monk felt the weight of his brush anew. He was not merely painting an image—he was bringing a sacred world into being.

The Arrival of Tantrism in Tibet: The Journey of Padmasambhava

"Who brought these images to Tibet?" the monk asked, looking up from his work.

The master's gaze flickered toward the ancient altar, where a statue of Padmasambhava—Guru Rinpoche—stood in fiery splendour.

"Guru Rinpoche," the master said with deep reverence. "The one who tamed the spirits and sowed the seeds of Vajrayana Buddhism in Tibet."

In the 8th century, Tibet was a land of fierce mountain spirits and ancient Bon rituals. Buddhism had begun to take root, but it struggled against the forces of the old world. The king, Trisong Detsen, knew that only a master of extraordinary power could subdue the wild energies of Tibet and establish the Dharma.

Padmasambhava arrived, wielding not just knowledge but the force of Tantric transformation. He did not destroy the old gods—he transformed them, weaving them into the new faith as protectors and guides. His teachings shaped the very foundations of Tibetan Buddhism, turning monasteries into sanctuaries of esoteric wisdom and art into a path of awakening.

Nepal, Bhutan, Tibet, and Ladakh: The Four Pillars of Tantric Art

The young monk dipped his brush into gold paint and traced the flames surrounding the deity on his canvas. "And what of Nepal, Bhutan, and Ladakh?" he asked.

His master's voice took on the rhythm of an ancient tale, shaped by centuries of whispered prayers. "Each land shaped Tantric art in its own way, yet all remained connected through the sacred thread of Vajrayana."

Nepal: The Birthplace of Vajrayana Art

The sacred valleys of Kathmandu, Patan, and Bhaktapur became home to the Newar artisans, whose hands could bring gods to life. Their metalwork, thangkas, and stupas were unparalleled in their intricacy. It was here that many of the images now revered in Tibet were first created, carried across the mountains by pilgrims and scholars.

Nepali artists perfected the mandala, sacred diagrams mapping the cosmic order, and crafted statues so lifelike they seemed to breathe. Even today, their work fills the monasteries of Tibet and Bhutan, unbroken by time.

Tibet: The Realm of the Cosmic Dance

In Tibet, Tantric Buddhism found its true kingdom. Temples and caves became living mandalas, their walls alive with guardian deities, peaceful Buddhas, and wrathful protectors. Every painting, every sculpture was a doorway into enlightenment, a coded language of symbols meant to guide the seeker beyond illusion.

The wrathful deities were not demons—they were forces of compassion in disguise, tearing apart ignorance with divine fury. Even the Yab-Yum figures, gods and goddesses locked in embrace, were not about passion but the union of wisdom and emptiness.

Bhutan: The Keeper of Sacred Traditions

Bhutan, a kingdom of hidden valleys and towering dzongs, became the guardian of Tantric purity. The fortresses of Bhutan were not just castles, but monasteries, where monks spent lifetimes painting sacred murals and whispering powerful mantras.

Even today, Bhutanese temples glow with the same vibrant colors and golden deities that once adorned ancient scrolls. The spirit of Vajrayana has remained untouched, alive in the whispers of the mountains.

Ladakh: The Himalayan Crossroads of Tantric Art

Ladakh, the northernmost region of India, sits at the confluence of Tibetan and Indian Buddhist traditions. The great monasteries of Hemis, Thiksey, and Alchi serve as living museums of Vajrayana art.

The walls of Ladakh's temples are covered with detailed murals of the Wheel of Life, cosmic mandalas, and fierce Tantric deities. Ladakh's monks, following the Tibetan Buddhist tradition, continue to create thangkas and sand mandalas, preserving the teachings passed down through Padmasambhava.

The Eternal Brushstroke

As he lifted his brush to finish the thangka, the young monk realized that he was part of a lineage stretching back centuries, a lineage of hands that had painted, sculpted, and envisioned the divine.

The last stroke fell into place. A gateway had been opened—not just on the canvas, but within himself.

And as the butter lamps flickered, their light shimmering on golden deities and celestial forms, the temple whispered once more—a song of Tantra, of art, of wisdom passed through time.

> "Tantric Buddhist art is the visual embodiment of transformation—each intricate form a doorway to deeper spiritual realization."

A still life painting of Mask, Khukri and Vajra

BUDDHIST ENGINEERING AND ARCHITECTURE

11

THE ARCHITECT'S JOURNEY: HOW BLUEPRINTS AND CORE DESIGN MEASURES SHAPED BUDDHIST MONASTERIES AND TEMPLES

The wind carried the scent of damp earth as the young architect unrolled his parchment atop a wooden table. Before him stretched a vast, untouched landscape, destined to house a sacred monastery. His fingers traced the delicate lines of the blueprint—every arch, every pillar, every stone already set in his mind. Yet, this was not merely a structure of stone and wood; it was to be a bridge between the material world and the divine, a sanctuary where time itself would dissolve into meditation.

The elder monk, watching from the temple steps, stepped forward with slow, measured steps. He had seen many such plans over the years, but he understood that a true Buddhist sanctuary was more than walls and roofs. It was a vessel for the Dharma, a silent guide on the path to enlightenment.

The Sacred Geometry of Buddhist Architecture

"Look beyond the stones," the monk murmured. "A temple must breathe. It must mirror the universe."

The architect nodded. The blueprint of a Buddhist monastery was never arbitrary. It followed the shape of the cosmos itself, designed to guide the faithful from the distractions of the outer world into the stillness of the inner self.

He studied the mandala—a sacred geometric pattern that would dictate the temple's entire layout. The courtyard, the meditation hall, the stupas—each piece placed in harmony with the other, forming a cosmic map of spiritual awakening.

The temple's entrance faced the east, where the first light of dawn would illuminate its path. The great vihara, or meditation hall, would sit in the west, where the setting sun would remind monks of impermanence. Every doorway, every corridor, every shadow cast by the setting sun had a purpose. Nothing was by chance.

Building a Path to Enlightenment

The architect walked the land, feeling the soil beneath his feet. He envisioned the great stupas, hemispherical domes symbolizing the enlightened mind. Some would house relics, others would simply stand as silent sentinels, reminding all who came here of the Buddha's teachings.

Within the monastery walls, he imagined the colonnaded pathways where monks would walk in meditation, their steps aligned with ancient chants. The corridors would be wide, open to the breeze, allowing the natural world to merge seamlessly with the spiritual realm. Nothing should feel confined, for the Dharma itself knows no boundaries.

The Legacy of Sacred Proportions

As his hand hovered over the blueprint, he recalled the lessons of ancient builders. The temples of Borobudur, Ajanta, and Angkor Wat—none were built haphazardly. Each structure followed sacred mathematical ratios, ensuring that the physical world resonated with divine harmony.

The stupa's height had to correspond to its width, creating perfect symmetry. The number of steps leading to the main hall represented the eightfold path. The towering pagodas, with their tiered roofs, symbolized ascension, drawing the eye and the soul toward Nirvana.

Even the monastery's water elements held meaning. Ponds were not merely for reflection; they represented the impermanence of all things, mirroring the changing sky above. Bridges over these waters were not just crossings but metaphors—the passage from ignorance to wisdom.

The Architect's Offering

Days passed, and the blueprint became more than ink on parchment—it became a story waiting to be told in stone and silence. The architect had designed structures before, but never had he felt the weight of creation in such a profound way. This temple would not just be built; it would be lived, breathed, and whispered into being through prayer and contemplation.

He turned to the elder monk. "Will this be worthy?" he asked.

The monk smiled, his eyes filled with years of wisdom. "Not all who walk these halls will seek enlightenment. But those who do, will find it. The walls will not teach them; the silence within them will." And so, with reverence, the architect placed his hands on the blueprint one last time before handing it over to the builders. The work had only just begun.

> "For a Buddhist monastery is not merely constructed—it is born, through intention, through devotion, through the quiet labor of many hands and many hearts."

12

BUDDHIST ENGINEERING CANONS: A STORY OF SACRED PRECISION AND MONUMENTAL INGENUITY

The sky was painted in hues of orange and gold as the sun dipped behind the towering spires of Borobudur. A group of monks and artisans stood before the grand structure, their eyes tracing the perfect symmetry of the stupa, the intricate carvings that adorned its stone walls, and the cosmic alignment that made it more than just a place of worship—this was a celestial machine in perfect harmony with nature.

Long before the first stone was laid, Buddhist engineers, guided by ancient wisdom and unwavering devotion, envisioned structures that would transcend time. Unlike the rigid architectural canons of Hindu temples, Buddhist construction principles were often passed down through oral traditions, inscribed in ancient Khmer texts, or detailed in the travelogues of Chinese monks who marveled at these engineering feats.

One such monk, Faxian, journeyed across the lands of Southeast Asia, chronicling the astonishing skill with which monasteries, stupas, and temples were crafted. He described the raised wooden structures of Thailand, perched on stilts to resist the floods that often swept through the lowlands. In Cambodia, he marveled at the massive sandstone blocks of Angkor Wat, interlocked so seamlessly without mortar that even the passing centuries could not break their embrace.

The secrets of these structures lay not just in their materials but in the profound understanding of their makers. **Blueprints, though rare, were etched in the minds of master builders**, who used manual sketches and wooden models to conceptualize their sacred designs. Every detail mattered—the alignment of a temple with the cardinal directions, the precise distribution of weight through interlocking stone blocks, and the inclusion of water reservoirs to sustain the surrounding communities.

As the monks and artisans of Bagan laid bricks with meticulous care, they understood that earthquakes would one day challenge their work. So, they devised **interlocking masonry techniques**, allowing their temples to sway with the tremors rather than collapse beneath them. In Indonesia, the builders of Borobudur embedded hidden drainage channels beneath the stupa, ensuring that even the heaviest monsoon rains could not erode its foundations.

One of the most fascinating aspects of Buddhist engineering was its ability to adapt to the landscape. **Himalayan monasteries clung to steep cliffs, their walls fortified with timber to absorb seismic shocks.** In the valleys of Myanmar, stupas were designed to mimic the lotus—wide, stable, and rooted deep into the earth. The Khmer architects of Cambodia engineered massive barays—artificial reservoirs that sustained entire temple cities, ensuring that both worshippers and the land itself thrived in perfect equilibrium.

The great stone faces of Bayon watched over the land, their expressions carved with serene wisdom, reflecting a civilization that understood not just the art of construction, but the philosophy of endurance. **Every temple, every stupa, every monastery was built not just for the present but for eternity, designed to withstand both time and the elements.**

Today, as conservationists and architects study these ancient marvels, they continue to uncover lessons in sustainable engineering—**from passive cooling techniques to earthquake-resistant design principles.** The Buddhist engineers of old did not merely build structures; they crafted legacies, blending spirituality with scientific mastery in a way that continues to inspire the world.

As the last rays of sunlight illuminated the intricate reliefs of Borobudur, a gentle breeze carried whispers of an ancient truth—**that in every stone, every arch, and every carefully placed brick, lay the wisdom of those who understood that true strength is not in resistance, but in harmony with the forces of nature.**

> "A Buddhist temple is not merely an architectural structure; it is a mandala in stone, a cosmic diagram guiding seekers toward inner peace."

A painting of a women at Boudhha at Katmandu, Nepal

13

BUDDHIST ENGINEERING IN ROCK-CUT CAVES: A TALE OF STONE AND SPIRIT

The echoes of chisels against stone once filled the air as the master artisan surveyed the towering cliffs before him. The monks stood behind him in quiet anticipation, their robes billowing in the wind, as they contemplated the immense task before them. This mountain, unyielding and vast, was to become a place of refuge—a monastery carved not with timber and mortar, but with devotion, patience, and the precision of engineering genius.

Carving a sanctuary into solid rock was no ordinary feat. The artisans of ancient India, Afghanistan, and Sri Lanka understood that to build something that would withstand centuries, they would have to work with the mountain, not against it. **Their first lesson: choosing the right rock.** Basalt, granite, and sandstone cliffs were selected for their stability, ensuring the longevity of their sacred halls. These monks were not only spiritual seekers but engineers who saw beyond the stone, envisioning corridors and prayer halls within the very fabric of the earth itself.

The first step in their laborious endeavor was to weaken the rock, making it easier to carve. They knew the secret that water, over time, could soften even the hardest stone. Water was poured into natural cracks, seeping deep into the rock's core. As the mountain drank, the rock swelled and weakened, allowing the chisels and hammers to carve away at its layers with newfound ease. **Water was not just an element—it was an instrument.**

The artisans began their work from the top, carving downward, ensuring gravity would aid them rather than hinder them. This technique, used at Ajanta and Ellora in India, prevented debris from collapsing inward, preserving the delicate interior murals and sculptures. With each strike of the chisel, the mountain yielded magnificent chaitya halls, prayer rooms, and vast networks of monastic cells. The walls bore intricate murals of the Buddha's past lives, their pigments drawn from crushed minerals, bound with time itself.

But carving stone was only part of the challenge. How would light illuminate the vast interiors, where monks would gather to meditate in solitude? **Natural and artificial lighting played a crucial role in their designs.** Skylights and doorways were strategically placed to capture the sun's shifting path, while stone niches were carved into walls to hold flickering oil lamps, casting long shadows against frescoed walls.

Water, the very element that had softened the stone for carving, was also revered in these sanctuaries. Rainwater collection systems, ingeniously designed, ensured that no monastery was ever without a sustainable source of water. At Dambulla in Sri Lanka, hidden reservoirs collected the monsoon rains, while in the arid lands of Bamiyan, underground channels brought life-giving water from distant sources. **These caves were not just refuges for monks—they were self-sustaining worlds within the mountain.**

At the famed **Bamiyan Caves in Afghanistan**, artisans carved massive Buddha statues directly into the cliffs, towering over the valley below. Pilgrims and traders on the Silk Road gazed up in awe at the figures, their painted robes seemingly caught mid-motion in the wind. The caves behind them were adorned with oil-based murals—an innovation centuries ahead of its time.

In India, **Ajanta and Ellora became masterpieces of Buddhist rock-cut architecture**, their stone corridors resonating with silent chants. The ceilings, curved like wooden temples, were etched with lotus motifs, while massive stone pillars held up halls large enough to hold a hundred monks in prayer. Every surface told a story—the birth of the Buddha, his teachings, his journey toward enlightenment. Meanwhile, in Sri Lanka, **the Dambulla Cave Temple** stood as an oasis of tranquillity. With over 150 statues of the Buddha resting in the embrace of natural rock, the monastery remained cool in the sweltering heat, its thick stone walls offering insulation long before the concept of climate control was understood.

As the centuries passed, earthquakes rattled the land, empires rose and fell, and invaders sought to erase what they did not understand. Yet, the caves stood firm, their monolithic nature granting them resilience against both nature and man. Today, modern engineers and architects look back at these rock-cut marvels with admiration, seeking inspiration for sustainable designs. Their methods—**passive cooling, water conservation, and seismic-resistant architecture**—hold valuable lessons for a world grappling with environmental and structural challenges. The last chisel strike was made centuries ago, but the wisdom embedded in these sacred sanctuaries remains eternal. The mountains may have given way to the hands of the monks, but in return, those who carved them left behind more than stone—they left behind a legacy, etched into the heart of the earth itself.

> "Water sustains life, but in Buddhist engineering, it also sustains wisdom—flowing through stupas, monasteries, and sacred spaces as a metaphor for impermanence."

14

BUDDHIST ENGINEERING IN DISASTER-PRONE REGIONS: A STORY OF MONASTIC RESILIENCE

The mountain air was crisp as the monks of Thiksey Monastery gathered before dawn, their breath forming small clouds in the cold Ladakhi sky. Nestled high in the Himalayas, the monastery had stood for centuries, its walls witnessing the tremors that shook the valley and the storms that battered its stone foundations. Yet, through earthquakes and time, it remained—a silent guardian of wisdom, a testament to the ingenuity of Buddhist engineering.

In the heart of the Himalayas, where tectonic forces clashed beneath the surface, Buddhist monks had long understood the power of nature. They had seen valleys split open, watched mountains tremble, and felt the earth groan beneath their feet. But instead of fearing these forces, they studied them, crafting monasteries that could bend without breaking, stand without crumbling. **Their secret? A delicate balance of flexibility and strength.**

At Thiksey and countless other monasteries across Nepal, Bhutan, and Tibet, the builders wove timber into the very fabric of their stone walls. The wood, unlike rigid stone, could flex, absorbing the force of seismic waves, preventing catastrophic collapse. **It was a lesson learned from nature itself—like the bamboo that bends in the wind but does not snap.**

Beyond the walls, the location of the monastery was never an accident. The monks chose their sites with care, seeking the embrace of bedrock, away from the dangers of landslides and floods. They built low-rise structures, layered like the mountains themselves, stepping in harmony with the slopes. Their windows remained small, their walls thick, each detail calculated to withstand the fury of the trembling earth.

Yet, not all Buddhist monks lived in the shadow of earthquakes. In the volcanic lands of Indonesia and Myanmar, another battle was fought—not against shifting earth, but against fire and ash. Here, too, Buddhist architects had mastered resilience.

The towering stupas of Borobudur in Indonesia stood as proof, their pyramid-like structures dispersing energy from tremors, their interlocking stone blocks shifting just enough to absorb shocks. Made of volcanic andesite rock, quarried from the very mountains that threatened them, these temples embraced their environment rather than resisting it. Even as ash rained from distant eruptions, the stone endured, impervious to time and fire.

The monks understood that water was just as powerful a force as fire. Around the golden Shwedagon Pagoda in Myanmar, they carved intricate drainage channels, ensuring that monsoon rains and volcanic ash never pooled to weaken their foundations. In Java, they built their monasteries on elevated ground, ensuring lava flows would bypass their sacred halls.

Through centuries of trial and wisdom, Buddhist monks across disaster-prone regions had perfected the art of survival. **They did not fight against nature—they worked with it.** They used the earth's gifts—timber, stone, water—to craft temples that could stand the test of time, balancing resilience with reverence for the land.

Today, as modern cities battle earthquakes and volcanic eruptions, there is much to learn from these ancient builders. Their understanding of flexible materials, strategic site selection, and water management holds valuable lessons for architects striving to create disaster-resistant communities.

As the morning light crested over the Himalayas, the monks of Thiksey Monastery began their chants, their voices echoing through halls that had seen centuries of quakes, storms, and trials. And yet, the monastery stood firm—**not as a relic of the past, but as a guide for the future.**

> "To build an earthquake-resistant monastery is to understand the deepest truth of Buddhism—impermanence is inevitable, but wisdom is adaptable."

15

THE STUPA AND THE VOLCANO: BOROBUDUR'S SACRED BALANCE WITH FIRE

In the heart of Central Java, surrounded by lush jungle and rice fields that shimmer in the morning mist, a sacred mountain of stone rises—silent, steady, and mysterious. Borobudur, the world's largest Buddhist stupa, was not born from conquest or ego, but from contemplation and cosmic balance. And not far from its sacred silence looms a force of fire and fury—Mount Merapi, one of the most active volcanoes in the world.

To the untrained eye, they may seem like opposites. One erupts; the other meditates. But in Javanese spiritual consciousness, they are part of the same story—a dance between impermanence and transcendence.

When Borobudur was built in the 8th–9th century by the Shailendra dynasty, its architects were not merely constructing a monument; they were sculpting a cosmic mandala from volcanic stone. Rising like a lotus from the earth, its nine stacked platforms and central stupa mirror the path of enlightenment. But its placement was not just geographical—it was spiritual. Mount Merapi lies directly to its north, and ancient cosmology saw this alignment as no coincidence. Fire above, water below—the Indian Ocean to the south. In between stood Borobudur, a sacred bridge between destruction and renewal.

Some believe Borobudur was constructed not to resist the volcano's wrath but to coexist with it. In a culture where natural elements were seen as deities, Merapi was not an enemy but a teacher—one whose unpredictable power reminded humanity of life's fragile beauty. Borobudur's existence, then, became a prayer in stone, a spiritual equilibrium to Merapi's fire. Where Merapi erupts, Borobudur absorbs; where Merapi transforms, Borobudur transcends.

Each of Borobudur's 504 Buddha statues faces outward, gazing into space with serenity. Some are enshrined within perforated stupas—meditating within stone lattices that blur the line between visibility and mystery. These Buddhas are not identical; they each express a different mudra, or symbolic gesture—meditation, teaching, fearlessness, generosity. And yet, together, they form a unified field of awakening, guiding pilgrims through the stages of spiritual evolution.

Pilgrims begin at the base, among carvings that depict worldly desire, chaos, and craving—the realm of kāmadhātu. As they ascend the stone corridors in clockwise circumambulation, they walk into the rūpadhātu, where over 1,400 relief panels tell the life of the Buddha, the Jataka tales, and the cycles of samsara.

Then, reaching the open terraces of the arūpadhātu, all carvings fall away. There is no story left to tell. Only space. Stillness. Sky.

This journey was not symbolic alone. It was a ritual, a spiritual ascent—a mirror of one's inner transformation. And it was made all the more powerful by the volcano nearby. For in Borobudur's sacred silence and Merapi's fierce roar, devotees understood that life contains both—the meditative and the explosive, the grounded and the uncontrollable.

When Merapi erupted, people did not abandon Borobudur. They returned, walking its platforms in the ash-scented air. They understood the message etched in its volcanic stones: nothing is permanent—not even destruction. The volcano speaks of death; the stupa responds with rebirth.

Borobudur was not built to stop the volcano—but to honor it. Not to control nature—but to live in balance with it. Its very construction from volcanic rock—stone that once flowed molten from Merapi's core—was an act of transformation. Destruction turned into devotion. Chaos shaped into contemplation.

Even today, Borobudur stands not just as an archaeological wonder, but as a living prayer, a teaching etched in reliefs and silence. Artists study its symmetry. Engineers marvel at its interlocking structure, which has withstood centuries of quakes and eruptions. Pilgrims still walk its sacred path—rising from desire, through form, into formless peace.

And Mount Merapi still breathes.

Together, the stupa and the volcano remain—one in stone, the other in fire—each reminding us that the path to peace does not lie in resisting nature, but in understanding its rhythm. Borobudur is not just a monument; it is a message—of balance, of transformation, and of awakening amid impermanence.

It teaches not in words, but in form. Not in silence, but in sacred presence.

And its lesson, like the Buddha's, endures:

Even in the shadow of fire, there is a path to stillness.

16

BUDDHIST ENGINEERING IN WATER RESOURCE MANAGEMENT: A STORY OF HARMONY AND SUSTAINABILITY

The golden light of dawn shimmered on the surface of the monastery's sacred pond. A young monk knelt at the edge, cupping the cool water in his hands before bringing it to his lips. He watched as ripples expanded outward, dissolving into the stillness of the pool, mirroring the endless cycle of existence. Water, in Buddhist philosophy, was not just a necessity—it was a teacher, a symbol of purity, impermanence, and interconnectedness.

For centuries, Buddhist monks had learned to live in harmony with their environment, shaping the landscape not through force, but through wisdom. The monasteries they built in the highlands of Tibet, the valleys of Sri Lanka, and the volcanic fields of Indonesia were not only places of spiritual refuge but also masterpieces of sustainable water management. Each structure bore silent testimony to an understanding of water's power—its ability to give life, to carve mountains, and to shape civilizations.

At Nalanda, one of the greatest Buddhist universities of ancient India, engineers devised an intricate **rainwater harvesting system**, ensuring that monks and scholars never faced scarcity even in the driest seasons. Large reservoirs, linked by underground channels, collected rain during monsoons, preventing wastage and ensuring a year-round supply. The principles of conservation were woven seamlessly into daily life, a reminder that water was to be cherished, never squandered.

Farther south, in the heart of Sri Lanka, the **monastic city of Anuradhapura** stood as a marvel of Buddhist hydraulic engineering. Here, vast reservoirs, known as **wewas**, stretched like artificial lakes, feeding the rice fields and sustaining the community. These reservoirs, designed by monks and built by artisans, were more than just water storage units—they were ecosystems, sustaining both human and animal life. Lotus flowers bloomed on their surfaces, cooling the water and preventing algae growth, while carefully constructed spillways controlled the ebb and flow, protecting the land from devastating floods.

In the towering mountains of Tibet and Nepal, where glaciers whispered their ancient secrets, Buddhist monks mastered **gravity-fed irrigation systems**. At **Drepung Monastery**, perched high in the Himalayas, water from melting ice was carefully directed through stone channels, ensuring a steady flow into temple courtyards and village farms below. Even at these dizzying heights, water was never taken for granted. Each drop that traveled through these sacred corridors was revered, its journey a reflection of the impermanence that Buddhist monks contemplated in their daily meditations.

But the monks of Southeast Asia faced a different challenge. Here, the land trembled under the shadow of volcanoes, and torrential rains could wipe out entire settlements in a matter of hours. At **Borobudur**, one of the world's greatest Buddhist monuments, engineers built with foresight. Using volcanic andesite stone, they constructed a stupa complex designed not just to endure the region's seismic tremors, but also to manage its unpredictable rains. Beneath its terraces, hidden channels redirected water safely away, preventing erosion and preserving the temple's intricate reliefs.

In the island temples of Bali, Buddhist monks coexisted with Hindu priests, creating a water-sharing system so sophisticated that it would one day be recognized as a UNESCO World Heritage site. The **Subak irrigation system**, guided by Buddhist principles of fairness and balance, ensured that water flowed from the mountains to the rice paddies below, feeding thousands in an unbroken cycle of abundance and gratitude.

Even today, as cities grow and resources dwindle, the lessons of Buddhist water engineering remain as relevant as ever. Across the world, architects and environmentalists look to ancient monasteries for inspiration—**to revive rainwater harvesting, restore natural wetlands, and rethink urban water conservation**.

As the young monk finished his morning ritual by the pond, he understood what his elders had always taught: **water was not just a resource—it was a responsibility**. The monasteries that had safeguarded it for centuries were more than places of worship. They were blueprints for a world where human ingenuity and nature existed not in opposition, but in perfect, fluid harmony.

A Sketch of Buddha visualised flying above from Bamiyan city in a watershed concept

THE POLITICAL AND IDEOLOGICAL IMPACT ON BUDDHIST ART

16

IMPACT OF THE COMMUNIST REGIME AND JUCHE PHILOSOPHY ON BUDDHISM AND ART IN NORTH KOREA: A STORY OF SUPPRESSION AND REINVENTION

The air was still in the ancient temple of Pohyonsa. Dust clung to the wooden pillars, where centuries-old carvings of the Buddha watched over an empty hall. The chants of monks had long since faded, replaced by the silence of a controlled state. Outside, a group of tourists admired the architecture, guided by officials who spoke not of enlightenment, but of preservation and cultural heritage—narratives carefully crafted to fit the state's ideology.

This was Buddhism in North Korea: a shadow of its past, a relic reshaped to serve a different master.

The Rise of Juche and the Fall of Buddhism

Before the Korean Peninsula was divided, Buddhism flourished in the temples and mountains of what is now North Korea. Monks walked in meditation through vast courtyards, scholars transcribed sacred sutras, and artisans carved intricate Buddha statues into rock faces. It was a world of devotion, art, and philosophy—until history intervened.

With the rise of Kim Il-sung and the founding of North Korea in 1948, Buddhism became an obstacle to the communist vision. Religion was a threat—an institution that encouraged faith beyond the Supreme Leader, a force that stood outside state control.

Temples were closed, monks were expelled or forced into labor, and centuries-old Buddhist artifacts were either destroyed or rebranded as national treasures devoid of spiritual significance. The government created the Korean Buddhist Federation (KBF), not as a religious institution, but as a mechanism of control, ensuring that whatever remained of Buddhism served the state's interests. The temples that survived were no longer places of worship but showcases of "Korean cultural identity" as approved by the regime.

Art Reimagined: From Spiritual Symbolism to State Propaganda

In the halls where once lay paintings of the Buddha's past lives, new murals emerged—glorious depictions of Kim Il-sung, heroic battle scenes, and workers striving toward self-reliance. The artistic traditions of North Korea did not die with Buddhism; they were reshaped under the doctrine of Juche, the philosophy of self-reliance that defined the nation's ideology.

Buddhist art, once a medium of spiritual transcendence, was transformed into a tool for political indoctrination. The deep folds of a Buddha's robe, inspired by Greco-Buddhist sculpture, were now seen in the stately uniforms of Kim Il-sung's portraits. The mandala's sacred geometry was repurposed into carefully arranged compositions glorifying the nation's military and economic aspirations.

The once-great frescoes of Korean temples, which had depicted celestial beings and Bodhisattvas, were either erased or altered, their figures replaced with scenes of the revolution, agricultural workers, and factories. Wooden carvings and sculptures that had once depicted Avalokiteshvara—the bodhisattva of compassion—were quietly removed, their places taken by busts of the Kim dynasty. Religion was gone, but the aesthetics of devotion remained—only now, they served the state.

The Temples That Survived: A Carefully Controlled Legacy

Pohyonsa, one of the few remaining Buddhist temples in North Korea, still stands—but it does not stand as a place of prayer. Instead, it is presented as a national landmark, an example of Korean cultural heritage. Visitors are guided through its ancient halls, but no monks remain to perform rituals.

Other temples, like those in Kaesong and Mount Myohyang, have been restored, but not for religious revival—they serve as diplomatic tools, carefully maintained to present North Korea as a preserver of its own history, even as it has erased the faith that once thrived there.

For the few monks who still exist within this tightly controlled system, Buddhism is practiced not as an act of faith but as an obligation to the state. Their roles are ceremonial, their words scripted. In the Juche ideology, the only acceptable devotion is to the leadership, and any form of spirituality must be subordinate to that loyalty.

The Artistic and Religious Future of North Korea

Today, Buddhism in North Korea exists only as a shell of its former self. It survives in stone carvings and empty temple halls, in the delicate brushstrokes of ancient paintings that have not yet been erased. But its heart—the prayers, the art, the spiritual devotion—is gone.

What was once a tradition of enlightenment has become a carefully curated museum piece, displayed when convenient, erased when necessary. In its place stands a new kind of faith—one not in the teachings of the Buddha, but in the absolute power of the regime.

And so, the stone Buddha watches over Pohyonsa, his face calm, unyielding, timeless. His lips are silent, but if he could speak, what would he say of the world that remains?

The Painting of a Myogil Buddha carved on rock in Kumgang Mountains in North Korea

> "In Buddhist art, power is not wielded through dominance, but through harmony—the brush is held by those who seek peace rather than control."

17

WHY BUDDHIST ART FORMS ARE STOLEN THE MOST: A STORY OF SACRED THEFT AND GLOBAL DEMAND

The rain fell lightly on the ancient stone walls of a secluded monastery in Nepal, where a lone monk lit incense before a towering Buddha statue. He bowed in silent reverence, unaware that in the shadows of the temple, a group of thieves had already marked the relic for removal. By morning, the statue would be gone, another sacred artifact lost to the insatiable hunger of the global art market.

This scene, though fictional, is one that has played out in countless temples, monasteries, and archaeological sites across Asia. Buddhist art, with its spiritual gravity and exquisite craftsmanship, has become one of the most stolen cultural heritages in history. But why is it so frequently looted, and who fuels this demand?

The Vulnerability of Buddhist Art

For over two millennia, Buddhist artisans have sculpted, painted, and cast breathtaking images of the Buddha and Bodhisattvas. From the sandstone carvings of India's Sanchi Stupa to the golden Buddhas of Thailand's Ayutthaya temples, these creations were meant for devotion, not trade. Yet, across centuries, their sacred forms have been plundered, fragmented, and shipped across continents.

1. The Silence of Isolated Monasteries
   Many Buddhist temples sit in remote areas, guarded only by monks who dedicate their lives to meditation rather than security. The lack of modern protection makes these sites easy targets for looters, who can slip away unnoticed under the cover of night.
2. The Ghost of Colonialism
   During the 19th and 20th centuries, European collectors took Buddhist relics as trophies of empire, displaying them in museums from London to Paris. Temples in India, Sri Lanka, Cambodia, and Tibet were looted, their sculptures and frescoes stolen under the guise of "preserving history." Even today, stolen relics from that era sit in the grand halls of Western institutions, detached from their spiritual homes.
3. War and Religious Persecution
   The modern age has not been kinder. In Tibet, during the Chinese occupation, thousands of monasteries were razed, and their sacred thangkas, bronze sculptures, and scriptures disappeared into underground markets. In Afghanistan, the destruction of the Bamiyan Buddhas in 2001 was preceded by

decades of smaller-scale looting, where relics from Buddhist caves found their way to black-market buyers in Hong Kong and Tokyo.

4. The Lucrative Trade in Buddhist Art
   Buddhist sculptures fetch astronomical prices on the global stage. Auction houses in New York and London regularly sell centuries-old Buddha statues for millions, often without verifying their origins. Smugglers forge documentation, passing stolen relics through layers of dealers until they appear "legitimate." Meanwhile, elite collectors, enthralled by the mystique of the East, pay fortunes to own a piece of Buddhist antiquity.

Where Are These Artifacts Stolen From?

- **India and Nepal**: The sacred sites of **Nalanda, Ajanta, and Lumbini** have been stripped of statues, murals, and even temple doors.
- **Tibet and China**: The looting of Tibetan monasteries has led to countless lost thangkas, bronze figures, and relics appearing in European galleries.
- **Cambodia and Thailand**: Khmer Empire ruins, including **Angkor Wat**, have been systematically plundered, while Thailand's temples have lost golden Buddhas to international buyers.
- **Afghanistan**: Before the Taliban's destruction of the Bamiyan Buddhas, smaller statues and carvings had already been smuggled out, hidden in crates labeled as "household goods."

The Demand for Sacred Objects

1. **Western Museums and Collectors**
   Private collections in the West are filled with **"exotic" Buddhist sculptures**, seen as symbols of enlightenment. Museums, including the **British Museum and The Met**, house vast collections of Buddhist relics—some acquired under questionable circumstances.
2. **Wealthy Spiritual Enthusiasts**
   The rise of Buddhism in Western wellness culture has fueled an ironic trend—**affluent seekers of peace and mindfulness purchasing stolen Buddha statues as home décor**. For them, these artifacts symbolize tranquility; for Buddhist monks, their theft represents a tragic spiritual severance.
3. **Black Markets and Underground Traders**
   Smugglers transport relics through **Bangkok, Hong Kong, and Tokyo**, forging documents to mask their illicit origins. Many items end up in high-end antique shops, waiting for buyers unaware—or indifferent—to their dark histories.

Fighting Back: The Repatriation of Stolen Heritage

1. **International Agreements**
   In 1970, **UNESCO passed the Convention on Cultural Property**, calling for the return of stolen artifacts. Yet, enforcement remains weak, and black-market trade continues.
2. **Government Crackdowns**
   Nations like **India, Nepal, and Cambodia** have begun reclaiming their stolen heritage. Several high-profile cases have seen smuggled Buddha statues returned, though the process is often slow and fraught with legal battles.

3. **Ethical Museum Practices**
   Facing mounting pressure, **institutions like The Met and the British Museum** have started investigating the provenance of their Buddhist artifacts. Some relics have been returned, but many remain in glass cases, far from the lands they were meant to bless.

A Future of Awareness and Protection

As the monk in the temple gazed at the empty pedestal where the Buddha once stood, he sighed. The statue was not just stone; it was a vessel of wisdom, a guide for seekers. Its theft was more than a loss of art—it was a spiritual wound.

Buddhist artifacts continue to vanish into the hands of the wealthy, but the tide is shifting. Awareness is growing, governments are taking action, and voices are rising to demand that these sacred relics be returned to their rightful homes.

For the monks who pray in empty temples, and for the cultures seeking to reclaim their stolen past, the battle is not just about art—it is about identity, respect, and the right to preserve their spiritual heritage. The Buddha belongs not in a collector's vault but in the sanctuaries where he has guided generations toward enlightenment.

> *"When a Buddhist artifact is stolen, it is not only an object that is lost, but a spiritual bridge severed from its sacred origins."*

19

THE BRUSHSTROKES OF COMPASSION: A STORY OF ART, BUDDHA, AND CHRIST

The temple's dimly lit chamber smelled of ancient parchment and fresh paint. A young artist sat cross-legged before a stretched silk canvas, his brush hovering above the serene face of Avalokiteshvara. His hands were steady, yet his heart wavered. Today, he was to complete the eyes—the soul of the painting. His master, an old monk with a voice as soft as the rustling prayer flags outside, watched over him.

The young artist hesitated. "Master," he asked, "How does one paint compassion?"

The old monk chuckled, stepping forward to examine the near-completed thangka. "Compassion is not something you paint, child. It is something you see, something you feel. Do you know why Avalokiteshvara has a thousand arms?"

The young artist swallowed and nodded. "To reach all beings in suffering."

The master smiled. "Yes, and each hand carries a tool—not for war, not for conquest, but for healing, for guiding, for protecting. This is the compassion of the Buddha. It is not loud, it does not demand, but it is always present."

The young artist looked back at the divine figure before him. Avalokiteshvara's face bore an expression of infinite kindness, his many hands stretched outward, offering protection, wisdom, and peace. Every line of his form was a whisper of love.

Compassion in Buddhist Art: The Silence of Wisdom

For centuries, artists had captured compassion in Buddhist art—not as suffering, but as boundless serenity. Buddha's half-closed eyes did not weep, they watched, ever-aware of human suffering. His lips did not cry out in sorrow, they curled into a faint smile, reminding seekers that peace was within reach.

The Bodhisattvas, those who chose to remain in the world rather than ascend to Nirvana, embodied a different kind of love. Unlike Buddha, who transcended suffering, they stood at the threshold, ready to guide others forward.

In the temples of Nepal, Tibet, and China, Avalokiteshvara took form in elaborate murals and statues, his many eyes scanning the suffering of the world. In China, he became Guanyin, the motherly goddess of mercy, her arms cradling the sick and the lost.

Mandalas, the intricate geometric art of Buddhist tradition, carried the same silent message. Compassion was not a moment of pity; it was an eternal force, a design woven into the fabric of existence.

A Question of Difference: How Does Christ's Compassion Compare?

The young artist, still deep in thought, dipped his brush into gold pigment, preparing to complete the eyes of the deity. But something lingered in his mind. "Master," he said after a long silence, "How is this compassion different from the love spoken of by Jesus Christ?"

The old monk sat beside him, folding his hands. "It is different in expression, but not in essence."

"Buddha's compassion is like the moon—always present, always watching, but distant. Jesus Christ's compassion is like fire—burning, consuming, willing to suffer alongside those in pain."

The Passion of Christ: The Art of Suffering

In Buddhist art, suffering is acknowledged but never dominates the composition. But Christian art—especially that of the Renaissance and Baroque periods—depicts compassion through visible suffering.

Where Avalokiteshvara's hands reach outward, Jesus' hands are nailed to the cross, bloodied and broken. His face does not remain still in meditative calm, but contorts in agony.

Buddhist compassion is tranquil, like a vast ocean, guiding one to enlightenment. Christian compassion is visceral—it carries the weight of suffering, it bleeds, it sacrifices.

In paintings of Christ's Pietà, the Virgin Mary cradles the lifeless body of her son, her sorrow raw and human. Where Buddhist art teaches detachment from pain, Christian art leans into it, making suffering the bridge between humanity and the divine.

Two Paths, One Destination

The young artist placed the final brushstroke, completing Avalokiteshvara's golden eyes. The deity gazed outward, not in sorrow, not in joy, but in infinite presence. The artist sat back, his heart light with understanding.

"Buddha and Christ," the master murmured, "Both are paths of compassion. One watches over suffering with peace, the other walks into it with open arms. But in the end, both lead to the same truth."

The young artist bowed his head in respect. The temple bells rang in the distance, their echoes carrying the whispers of prayers and ages of wisdom. He had learned a lesson beyond the strokes of a brush—that compassion, in all its forms, is the art of the divine.

> "Compassion in Buddhist art is not just an expression of kindness; it is the artistic embodiment of wisdom and the interconnectedness of all beings."

A practicing monk

SYMBOLISM AND IMPERMANENCE IN BUDDHIST ART

20

IN THE SILENCE OF STONE: THE BAMIYAN BUDDHAS AND THE ECHO OF IMPERMANENCE

Long ago, in a wind-carved valley high in the heart of the Hindu Kush, two great sentinels stood watch over the Silk Road. Carved into the ochre cliffs of Bamiyan, in present-day Afghanistan, these colossal Buddhas—one 38 meters tall, the other soaring to 55—rose not from ambition or empire, but from devotion.

They were not merely statues. They were prayers in stone, embodiments of compassion and serenity carved directly into the mountain, overlooking travellers and monks who passed below, whispering mantras into the wind.

For centuries, these Buddhas of Bamiyan stood unshaken—through shifting dynasties, the spread of Islam, and the slow retreat of Buddhism from the region. Their creators, likely 6th-century Mahayana Buddhists under Kushan influence, drew upon Greco-Buddhist artistic traditions inherited from Gandhara. Their robes were carved with flowing drapery; their features serene, eternal. Their gaze stretched far beyond the valley—watching not with eyes, but with presence.

The stone around them bloomed with monastic caves, chaityas, and vibrant murals—some said to be the earliest known oil paintings in the world. Pilgrims once climbed hidden stairways within the statues themselves, ascending as if through the spine of the Buddha, emerging through windows at shoulder height, as if to look out through enlightened eyes.

But impermanence is the heartbeat of Buddhism.

And even mountains are not immune to time.

Centuries later, on a March day in 2001, the world watched in horror as dynamite and artillery reduced these giants to dust. The Taliban, in an act of iconoclastic violence, destroyed not only the statues—but a part of the world's shared spiritual heritage.

Yet the message of the Bamiyan Buddhas did not die. It deepened.

Their destruction became a paradox—the physical loss illuminated their spiritual essence. In Buddhist philosophy, all things are transient: joy, sorrow, body, and even beauty carved in stone. The Buddha never asked to be worshipped in form, only in truth. The emptiness left behind became a living mandala, a reminder that clinging—even to monuments—is the root of suffering.

Today, the niches where the Buddhas once stood remain hollow, echoing with memory. Some call for reconstruction, others call for preservation of the void. Pilgrims still visit. Artists have projected light Buddhas into the empty alcoves, not to replace the originals, but to honor the absence—to let the loss become part of the story.

The Bamiyan Buddhas were born of stone but lived through spirit.

They were created in permanence, but now teach through impermanence.

They were symbols of strength, now symbols of fragility—and resilience.

As the wind moves through the hollow where the Buddha once stood, it carries no anger—only stillness. A stillness that tells us:

Even when the form is gone, the truth remains.

The Graphite sketch of Bamiyan buddha ,Afghanistan

21

SACRED STROKES: THE TIMELESS BEAUTY AND MARKET VALUE OF BUDDHIST ANCIENT ART

The flickering candlelight cast shadows on the ancient murals, revealing the delicate brushstrokes that had survived centuries. In a dimly lit temple, nestled in the highlands of Tibet, an old monk traced the outlines of a fading thangka, his fingers gliding gently over the fabric as if whispering to the past. This painting, a masterpiece crafted by hands long gone, was more than an artistic expression; it was a sacred vessel carrying the wisdom of ages.

From the bustling auction halls of New York to the quiet prayer halls of Kyoto, Buddhist art has found itself at the crossroads of devotion and commerce. Once created to depict the life of the Buddha, his teachings, and the journey towards enlightenment, these ancient artworks have now become coveted treasures, sought after by collectors and museums worldwide.

The story of Buddhist art begins over 2,000 years ago, during the reign of Emperor Ashoka in India. At first, it was modest—silent, symbolic. The Buddha was represented not as a man but as a wheel, a tree, a footprint. Then, with the passage of time, as Buddhism spread along the Silk Road, his form emerged—first in Gandhara, where Greek and Indian artistic styles intertwined, and then in Mathura, where soft, rounded figures conveyed the warmth of spiritual serenity.

The journey of Buddhist art did not stop there. The grandeur of the Ajanta caves in India, the intricate temple carvings of Angkor Wat, the celestial murals of Dunhuang in China, and the towering stupas of Myanmar all became sacred landscapes where art met devotion. Each brushstroke, each chisel mark, held the weight of faith, a silent hymn to the enlightened one.

Yet, as centuries turned, the world began to see these sacred creations differently. No longer confined to temples and monasteries, Buddhist statues, thangkas, and carvings became objects of admiration and luxury. Collectors sought the serene faces of the Buddha, merchants transported statues across continents, and auction houses set record-breaking sales. A single thangka from the Yuan Dynasty, once a sacred offering, fetched $45 million in Hong Kong. A bronze Buddha, once enshrined in a monastery, found itself displayed in a Western museum.

But this transformation came with a price. Ancient monasteries in Nepal and Tibet saw their sacred relics vanish overnight, stolen and smuggled into private collections. Stone Buddhas, meant to guide worshippers, were chiseled away from temple walls and sold to the highest bidder. Nations fought to reclaim their heritage, while scholars debated the ethics of Buddhist art in foreign museums. Could a Buddha statue, removed from its temple, still serve its spiritual purpose?

Despite these challenges, Buddhist art continues to inspire. Even in a fast-changing world, the meditative strokes of a thangka, the delicate symmetry of a mandala, and the silent gaze of a stone Buddha remain reminders of a tradition that values impermanence, wisdom, and transcendence. Whether adorning a monastery or a collector's gallery, these masterpieces carry an eternal message—one that whispers through the ages, telling stories of faith, artistry, and the ever-evolving journey of Buddhist heritage.

> "The rivers of monastic architecture are not merely carved in stone; they flow with the wisdom of generations, carrying the past into the future."

The two young monks at Bouddha, Katmandu, Nepal

22

THE ETERNAL EPHEMERAL: A STORY OF THANGKA PAINTINGS, MANDALAS, AND THE ART OF IMPERMANENCE

The monastery stood on the edge of a great cliff, overlooking a valley where the clouds seemed to dance with the golden rays of the setting sun. The chants of monks echoed through the stone corridors, blending seamlessly with the rustling of prayer flags, their colors faded by the passing of seasons. Inside one of the monastery's sacred chambers, a young apprentice knelt before a vast silk canvas, his breath shallow as his trembling hands hovered above the surface. He was about to begin his greatest challenge—to paint a Thangka, a visual embodiment of Buddhist teachings that had been passed down through generations. Every brushstroke had to be deliberate, every color imbued with meaning.

Behind him, his master watched in silence, an aged monk with a gaze as deep as the centuries. "Why do you hesitate, child?" the master finally asked.

The apprentice lowered his brush, his heart heavy. "Master, if everything fades, if nothing is meant to last, then why do we create at all?"

A knowing smile flickered across the old monk's lips. "Because, child, impermanence is not a curse—it is a truth."

The Art of Thangka: A Canvas for the Fleeting

The apprentice's fingers tightened around his brush, yet the weight of his question lingered. His master, sensing his struggle, gestured toward the half-finished Thangka before them. It was a breathtaking sight, even in its incomplete form—Avalokiteshvara, the Bodhisattva of Compassion, his many arms reaching out to the suffering of the world.

"A Thangka is not just a painting," the master continued. "It is a reflection of life itself. Every stroke, every hue is a whisper of wisdom. But like all things, it will fade—perhaps in a century, perhaps in mere moments. That does not make it meaningless. It makes it sacred."

The apprentice listened in silence, his doubts still present but softened by the depth of his master's words. He had spent years watching the elder monks create these masterpieces, their steady hands never faltering, their devotion unwavering. But it had always puzzled him—why pour so much effort into something that time would eventually claim?

Mandalas: The Universe in Motion

His thoughts were interrupted by the soft sound of sand shifting. In the great hall, another sacred ritual was unfolding—the creation of a sand mandala. A group of monks worked in perfect harmony, pouring grains of vibrant sand onto a vast circular canvas. Hours turned to days as they meticulously shaped geometric patterns, symbols of the cosmos and the impermanence of existence.

The apprentice turned to his master, his curiosity rekindled. "And the mandala?"

The old monk gestured toward the intricate design. "Watch."

Days later, as the mandala neared completion, the apprentice marveled at its perfection. The patterns seemed to vibrate with divine energy, their colors more vivid than any he had ever seen. But before he could fully appreciate its magnificence, the monks began to destroy it. With a single stroke, the delicate patterns were swept away, the colors collapsing into a formless blur of dust.

The apprentice gasped. "Why?" he whispered, his voice barely audible. "Why create something so perfect, only to destroy it?"

The master placed a gentle hand on his shoulder. "Because nothing is perfect. And nothing is permanent."

The Role of Buddhist Monks in Preserving, Conserving, and Promoting Art

The apprentice followed his master down the winding corridors of the monastery, his mind still reeling from the lesson he had just witnessed. The walls were adorned with murals that had stood for centuries, their colors softened by time but their stories as powerful as ever. The old monk gestured toward them. "These works exist because of the hands that preserve them, because of the monks who dedicate their lives to ensuring that their wisdom endures."

The apprentice listened intently, realizing that the role of the monks extended far beyond the act of creation. They were the guardians of a timeless tradition, keepers of stories that would have otherwise been lost to the winds of change.

Monks serve as the protectors of sacred art, maintaining the intricate paintings and sculptures within temples.

They train apprentices, ensuring that the artistic traditions of Thangkas, sculptures, and architectural wonders do not fade into obscurity.

Through their art, they teach Dharma, using visual storytelling to inspire and educate generations.

They restore ancient murals and manuscripts, bringing back the vibrancy of forgotten masterpieces.

They promote Buddhist art beyond monastery walls, sharing its teachings with the modern world through exhibitions, collaborations, and digital archives.

The apprentice's heart swelled with newfound understanding. He had always thought of art as something one created, but now he saw the larger picture—art was also something one nurtured, protected, and ultimately let go.

The Role of Buddhist Murals and Frescoes in Spiritual Storytelling

The master then led the apprentice to the monastery's main hall, where grand frescoes covered the walls from floor to ceiling. Scenes of Buddha's past lives, celestial realms, and sacred teachings unfolded in layers of color and motion.

"Murals are not mere decoration," the master explained. "They are scriptures in form, narratives in light and shadow."

Murals depict the Jataka tales, stories of Buddha's past lives, offering moral lessons to devotees.

Frescoes serve as meditative aids, guiding monks and pilgrims into deeper contemplation.

They preserve historical events, ensuring the lineage and teachings of great Buddhist masters remain alive.

In monasteries where literacy was once rare, murals acted as visual sermons, educating entire communities.

The apprentice traced a delicate brushstroke along the robe of a painted Bodhisattva. Each line carried a lesson, each hue a fragment of wisdom. The realization settled within him—he was not merely an artist. He was a storyteller, a bridge between past and future.

The Final Stroke: A Lesson in Letting Go

Returning to his Thangka, the apprentice no longer hesitated. His brush moved with newfound confidence, weaving color and form into Avalokiteshvara's celestial expression. The painting was complete, but it would never be finished. Time would touch it, just as it touched all things, and one day it too would vanish.

But the wisdom it carried—the devotion it had inspired—that would remain, beyond paint, beyond silk, beyond form itself.

As he set down his brush, the final stroke placed, he felt a deep sense of peace. Outside, the wind carried away the last traces of the sand mandala, swirling colors dissolving into the earth. And in the heart of a young artist, the lesson of impermanence took root—not as loss, but as the very essence of life.

> "Thangka paintings are not mere artworks; they are visual prayers, each line infused with the meditative devotion of the artist."

> "A mandala is not meant to be possessed, but to be experienced—its dissolution is a lesson in the fleeting nature of all things."

The green Tara thangka painting

CONCLUSION AND REFLECTIONS

The painting of a Himalayan refugee from Tibet living in Katmandu

23

THE FUTURE OF BUDDHIST ART IN THE MODERN WORLD

The golden hues of dawn illuminated the ancient monastery, casting shadows that danced on the frescoed walls. Within its sacred halls, an artist traced the contours of a Thangka, his brush moving with the same reverence as generations before him. Yet, outside these walls, the world was changing, and Buddhist art was evolving along with it.

A Tradition in Transition

For centuries, Buddhist art remained rooted in tradition—delicate Thangka paintings, towering stupas, intricate mandalas, and serene Buddha sculptures shaped the spiritual landscape of monasteries across Asia. These works of art were not mere decorations; they were pathways to enlightenment, tools for meditation, and representations of the Dharma.

But today, the canvas of Buddhist art extends far beyond temple walls. It now breathes through digital screens, interactive exhibitions, and even artificial intelligence-generated imagery.

Modern artists are finding ways to honor tradition while embracing new mediums, allowing Buddhist art to reach audiences who may never step into a monastery.

Technology as a Bridge Between Past and Future

With the rise of virtual reality, 3D printing, and AI-generated art, the preservation and dissemination of Buddhist artistic heritage have entered a new era.

- **Digital Archives:** Ancient murals, some on the brink of decay, are now preserved in high-resolution digital formats, accessible to scholars and practitioners worldwide.
- **Virtual Reality Meditation Spaces:** Immersive VR experiences allow individuals to step inside long-lost temples or witness the sacred dance of Buddhist deities in digital form.
- **3D Printing and Restoration:** Temples damaged by time and natural disasters are being reconstructed using 3D modeling, ensuring that their sacred designs remain intact for future generations.

Yet, the question lingers—does the digitalization of Buddhist art diminish its sacred essence? Or does it offer new pathways for seekers to experience its transformative power?

The Contemporary Buddhist Artist

Today's Buddhist artists are not confined by the borders of tradition. They weave ancient symbols into contemporary paintings, infuse Buddhist teachings into modern street art, and even create multimedia installations that reflect the principles of impermanence and mindfulness.

In urban centers, galleries now feature abstract interpretations of Buddhist iconography, where minimalist brushstrokes evoke the stillness of Zen meditation. In contrast, graffiti artists in bustling cities use their craft to share messages of compassion and mindfulness, echoing the wisdom of the Dharma in unexpected places.

The Role of Buddhist Art in a Fragmented World

In an age of rapid change, where the world faces conflict, environmental crises, and spiritual disconnection, Buddhist art stands as a quiet refuge. It reminds us of interconnectedness, of impermanence, and of the deeper truths that transcend cultural and temporal boundaries.

- **Art as Activism:** Some contemporary Buddhist artists use their work to advocate for peace, environmental preservation, and social justice, merging spirituality with real-world concerns.
- **Public Art and Community Healing:** Murals depicting Buddha's teachings now grace hospitals, refugee centers, and rehabilitation spaces, offering solace to those in suffering.
- **Mindfulness in the Digital Age:** Interactive digital mandalas and AI-generated artworks encourage mindfulness in an age dominated by distractions.

Looking Ahead: The Endless Evolution

Buddhist art will continue to evolve, just as Buddhism itself has adapted over centuries. Whether through the strokes of a brush, the pixels of a digital screen, or the chisels of modern sculptors, the essence of Buddhist art remains unchanged—it is a conduit for wisdom, a means of connection, and a reminder of the transient beauty of existence.

As the artist in the monastery completes his Thangka, he looks beyond the temple walls. He knows that Buddhist art is no longer bound by geography or time. It is a living, breathing entity—endlessly becoming, just like the teachings it represents.

> "The future of Buddhist art does not seek to replicate the past, but to engage in a dialogue with it, ensuring its evolution with time."

24

IMPACT OF ARTIFICIAL INTELLIGENCE ON BUDDHIST ART FORMS

The temple stood silent, its ancient walls adorned with murals depicting the life of the Buddha. Monks in saffron robes moved through its corridors, chanting sutras as they had for centuries. But outside the monastery walls, the world was changing. A new artist had entered the sacred space of Buddhist art—**artificial intelligence**.

A New Brush in an Ancient Tradition

For thousands of years, Buddhist art has been shaped by human hands, guided by devotion and meticulous craftsmanship. Thangka painters spent years mastering their strokes, sculptors carved Buddha statues from stone with reverence, and mandala creators painstakingly constructed patterns only to destroy them as a lesson in impermanence. Now, AI-generated art is entering this sacred landscape, offering a new dimension to an age-old tradition.

With machine learning algorithms trained on centuries of Buddhist iconography, AI can now create intricate Thangka paintings in seconds, design mandalas with mathematical precision, and even generate virtual Buddhist sculptures that exist only in digital form. But does this innovation honor tradition, or does it challenge the very essence of Buddhist artistic practice?

The Intersection of AI and Buddhist Art

AI's role in Buddhist art can be seen in several ways:

- **Preservation of Ancient Works:** AI is being used to restore faded murals, reconstruct damaged statues, and analyze historical artworks with greater accuracy than ever before.
- **New Artistic Expressions:** Contemporary Buddhist artists are collaborating with AI to create interactive, evolving art pieces that reflect the principles of impermanence and interconnectedness.
- **Virtual Reality and Meditation Spaces:** AI-powered virtual Buddhist temples allow practitioners across the globe to experience sacred art without being physically present.

However, the question remains—does AI-generated Buddhist art carry the same spiritual essence as its human-made counterpart? Can a machine, devoid of devotion or mindfulness, truly create something sacred?

Philosophical and Ethical Considerations

Buddhism teaches that art is not about the artist but about the message it conveys. A statue of the Buddha is not revered for its material but for what it represents. If AI-generated art successfully transmits the teachings of the Dharma, does it matter whether it was made by a human or a machine?

Yet, there are concerns:

- **Loss of Human Connection:** Traditional Buddhist art involves deep meditation, devotion, and skill that AI lacks. Can an AI-created mandala evoke the same reverence as one crafted by a monk over weeks?
- **Commercialization of Sacred Art:** AI-generated Buddhist images risk being mass-produced, reducing the sacredness of unique, hand-crafted religious works.
- **Interpretation vs. Automation:** Human artists infuse their work with personal spiritual insights. AI, on the other hand, operates on data and patterns without understanding their deeper meanings.

The Future: Collaboration or Competition?

As AI becomes more sophisticated, Buddhist communities and artists face a crossroads. Rather than viewing AI as a threat, many are embracing it as a tool for innovation. Monks are using AI-generated art for teaching, digital artists are blending tradition with technology, and scholars are using AI to decode Buddhist symbols lost to time.

Perhaps the true future of Buddhist art lies not in choosing between human and AI creation, but in finding a balance between them. Just as Buddhism has adapted across cultures and centuries, its artistic expressions may also evolve, merging tradition with technology in ways yet to be discovered.

The monk in the temple looked at the digital Thangka displayed on a screen before him. It was stunning, precise, intricate. But as he turned to the old mural on the wall, weathered by time and brushstrokes of countless hands, he smiled. The old and the new were not enemies—they were simply different paths leading to the same truth.

> "Artificial intelligence may recreate the aesthetics of Buddhist art, but can it replicate the soul of devotion that breathes life into each piece?"

25

FINAL THOUGHTS: THE INTERSECTION OF SPIRITUALITY, ART, AND ENGINEERING

The monastery stood in the twilight, its golden spires catching the last embers of the setting sun. The wind carried the faint echoes of distant chants, blending with the rhythmic chisel strokes of an artist carving delicate patterns into the temple's wooden pillars. At the heart of this sacred space, where silence and devotion met craftsmanship, lay a truth often overlooked: that spirituality, art, and engineering were never separate pursuits, but rather, different expressions of the same human longing—for understanding, for beauty, for transcendence.

The Sacred Geometry of Faith

The young sculptor had spent years in apprenticeship, learning the precise calculations behind Buddhist stupas, the mathematical harmony of temple designs, and the fluid grace of Thangka paintings. He had always believed that spiritual art was an extension of faith, but he had come to realize something deeper—it was also an act of engineering, where devotion met structure, and belief was etched into stone and silk.

His master once told him, "Art and engineering are not just about creation; they are about continuity. A well-built monastery stands for centuries, just as a well-told story remains in the minds of generations." It was then he understood why ancient Buddhist artisans had sought balance in their creations—not just aesthetic balance, but structural, functional, and spiritual balance.

Art as a Bridge Between Worlds

In the great halls of Buddhist temples, murals did more than decorate walls. They told stories, preserved history, and guided monks through meditation. Each stroke of paint was an invitation, a pathway into the deeper truths of existence. The same applied to the towering stupas, where engineers aligned sacred structures with the movement of the stars, turning temples into celestial compasses that stood in harmony with nature.

A bridge connects two places, and Buddhist art was no different. It connected **past and future, faith and reason, the material and the metaphysical.** Engineers ensured that grand temples survived earthquakes, sculptors ensured that every curve of the Buddha's smile evoked compassion, and monks ensured that every creation remained faithful to the teachings of impermanence and wisdom.

The Eternal Ephemeral: A Lesson from Mandalas

The sculptor's mind drifted to the monks who spent days creating intricate mandalas, only to wipe them away in a single motion. At first, he saw this as an act of loss, but now he saw its purpose. **It was a reminder that all things—stone, silk, even faith itself—must change, evolve, and dissolve.**

He recalled the teachings of Buddhist monasteries across the Himalayas, where engineers and artists had to constantly rebuild temples against the force of time. Yet, each time they did, they added something new—a new pillar, a new painting, a new story. It was never the same monastery, yet it was always the same spirit.

The Future: The Convergence of Tradition and Innovation

As the sculptor placed the finishing touches on his work, he looked beyond the monastery to the world that lay ahead. The digital age had allowed ancient Buddhist art to be preserved in ways unimaginable to past generations. Virtual reality replicated the murals of long-lost caves, 3D printing allowed for the reconstruction of damaged statues, and modern architecture fused ancient designs with earthquake-resistant technology.

Yet, no matter how advanced these innovations became, the essence of Buddhist art and engineering remained unchanged. They were not merely about technique or form; they were about purpose, about ensuring that faith had a physical presence in the world.

The Final Reflection

The sculptor stood up, dusting his hands. His work was complete, but he knew it would never truly be finished. Time would touch it, just as it touched everything. But that was the beauty of it. **Art was never meant to last forever—it was meant to inspire, to be a moment of transcendence before being reclaimed by the universe.**

And so, with one final bow to his creation, he walked away, leaving behind something that would stand—not as a monument to permanence, but as a testament to the eternal cycle of creation, destruction, and rebirth.

> "Buddhist art, spirituality, and engineering are not separate disciplines but three interconnected paths leading to the same ultimate truth."

An old lady taking a bow at Buddha outside a temple

Thanking note from Author

As I reach the final pages of this book, I find myself filled with immense gratitude for the journey that has brought these stories to life. This work is not merely a collection of essays but a heartfelt exploration of Buddhist art, engineering, and philosophy—subjects that have shaped my travels, my reflections, and my understanding of the world.

First and foremost, I extend my deepest gratitude to the monks, scholars, artisans, and architects who have preserved the essence of Buddhist traditions for centuries. Their unwavering dedication to art and spirituality has been the foundation of this book, inspiring every word and every story. I am indebted to the masters of Thangka painting, the sculptors of Gandhara, the builders of Angkor Wat, and the countless unnamed creators whose hands have chiselled, painted, and carved the wisdom of the Dharma into tangible forms.I also wish to express my heartfelt appreciation to historians, researchers, and fellow travellers who have guided me in my exploration of Buddhist artistic and architectural marvels. Conversations with scholars, visits to ancient monasteries, and long discussions with monks have enriched my understanding and deepened my appreciation for the intersection of art and spirituality.

To my readers—whether you are an artist, a seeker, a historian, or simply someone drawn to the beauty of Buddhist art—I thank you. Your curiosity and openness to explore these themes make this journey all the more meaningful. I hope these narratives have not only provided insights into Buddhist artistic traditions but also inspired reflection on impermanence, devotion, and the ever-evolving dialogue between spirituality and creativity.

Finally, I extend my gratitude to the modern visionaries and digital preservers of art—those who are bringing ancient Buddhist art into the contemporary world through technology, artificial intelligence, and global exhibitions. The evolution of Buddhist art does not mark its end but ensures its continuity, allowing it to inspire generations to come.

This book is a tribute to all who have ever held a brush, carved a stone, designed a temple, or contemplated the delicate lines of a mandala. It is a tribute to the past, present, and future of Buddhist artistic expression.

With profound gratitude,

Rajkumar Gade

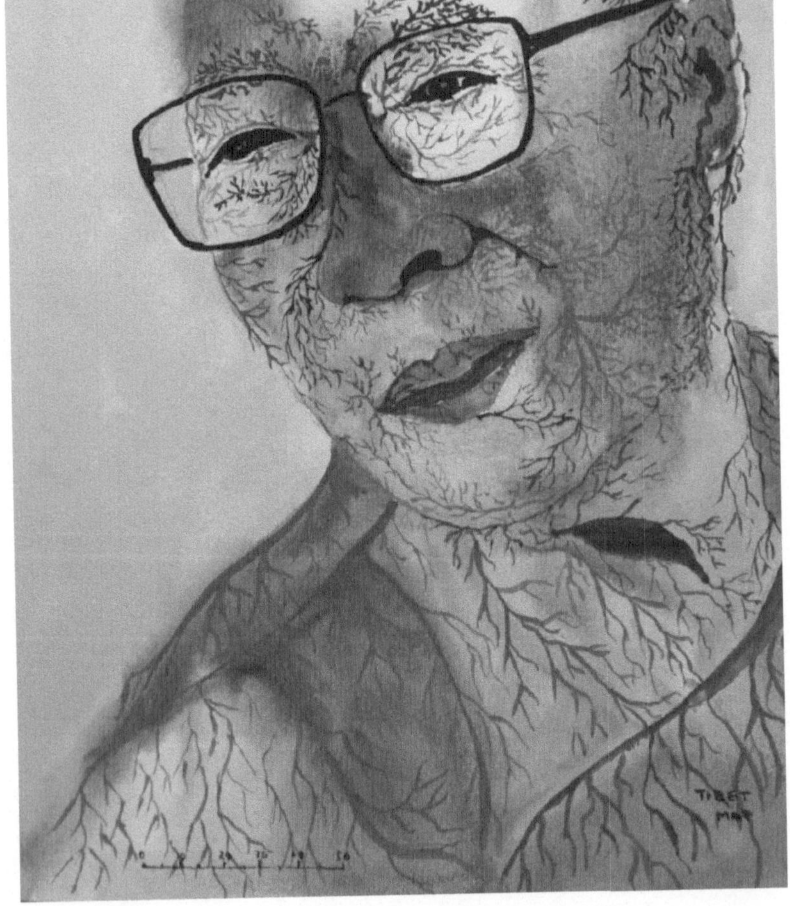

The Tibetan exiled Dalai lama painting visualised as a watershed